MERCILESS DEVIL

SONS OF VALENTINO, BOOK 2

KYLIE KENT

For Assunta
May every dark alley lead you to a Matteo of your own.
xx

Ebook ISBN: 978-1-922816-40-5
Paperback ISBN: 978-1-922816-55-9

Cover illustration by
Sammi Bee Designs

Editing services provided by
Kat Pagan – https://www.facebook.com/PaganProofreading

This book contains scenes of sexual acts, profanity, and violence. If any of these are triggers for you, you should consider skipping this read.

Savannah

Have you ever loved someone so much it physically hurts?

That's how much I love my best friend, Matteo Valentino.

It's also the reason I've done everything I can to make sure he's firmly rooted in the friend zone.

I'd rather keep him at a distance than ruin what we have by giving into the attraction constantly sparking between us.

That is until I wake up next to him with no recollection of how I ended up in his bed.

Matteo

When you're the prince of one of the five families of the New York mafia, nothing is off-limits.

That is until the one thing you want is your best friend.

Savannah St. James is everything light in my dark world.

She's strong, fierce, and more loyal than any made man I know.

She's also my best friend, and that makes her untouchable.

However, when I wake up next to her in Vegas after

a night out together, I'm not about to let her go as easily as she may think.

She'll find out just how merciless I am when it comes to keeping what I want.

And what I want, what I've always wanted, is *her*.

SAVANNAH

I have found the one whom my soul loves.

— Song of Solomon 3:4

S ome people spend their whole lives searching for their soul mate, their one true love. I found mine when I was only seven years old. I didn't know it at the time of course; all I knew was that the boy who stuck to my side like a shadow was different.

He wasn't like the other kids our age and I thought he was just silly. He liked to make people laugh. As we got older, I discovered that there was a lot more to Matteo Valentino. A lot more than he showed most people. And so much more than the happy, carefree persona he presented to the world. That version was all an act, an act the man deserves a damned Oscar for, because he plays that role so damn well sometimes even I forget it's fake.

Until we're alone, and the mask comes down. He never has to pretend with me, because no matter what, I will always have his back. We're more than just best friends; we are soul mates. Although I think the only one who had fantasies of us growing old together, getting married, and having babies… was *me*. Matteo is not the settling down kind of guy.

Even if he were, he's not the kind of guy I want to settle down with. The life he leads… well, let's just say I understand why my daddy tried to keep us apart when we were in grade school. It didn't work, obviously. Matteo and I have always been inseparable. A lot of people have tried to come between us, but that boy is nothing if not loyal.

I knew the extent of his loyalty when Johnny Valerie kissed me in the first grade. I tried to push him away but I wasn't strong enough. Matteo came up and tackled him, and seconds later, Matteo's older brother Theo was on top of Johnny too. The kid was left crying and bleeding on the ground. Without even a backwards glance, Matteo took my hand, walked me up to the corner store, and bought me a bag of candy.

He sat down with me and said, "Don't cry, Savvy. I'll never ever let anyone hurt you. I promise."

I shake my head, clearing the thoughts of the past

from my mind. Yes, I have found the one my soul loves, but it's not someone who will ever be anything more than my best friend. Not that we haven't ventured down a path of being more. We have. We were fifteen when we made a pact to lose our virginities to each other. It was a one-time thing, clumsy and awkward. And after the fact, I knew Matteo had the power to absolutely destroy me, break my heart into a million pieces, leaving nothing but an empty cavity in its spot. So to prevent that from happening, I ran.

I ran before he woke up the next morning. Ignored his calls all day until he broke into my bedroom window that night and forced me to talk to him. I made up some bullshit about how we had to stay friends and nothing more. Ever since then, I've pushed down my feelings for Matteo. I've told myself, and everyone else within earshot, that we are nothing more than friends. Best friends.

Judging by the six-foot-two solid mass of muscle currently sleeping in my guest bed while reeking of a brewery, we're also best friends who really shouldn't be sharing spare apartment keys. Those were my nice sheets, damn it. I'm probably going to have to burn them. If it wasn't for the empty bottle of Jack Daniels, the contents of which spilled onto the mattress, I could have salvaged the linens.

I kick my foot out, aiming for the leg that's hanging off the end of the bed. "Matteo Valentino, what the hell do you think you're doing?" I shout way louder than needed.

He groans, bringing a hand up to his face while squinting one eye open. He looks at me. "You're really pretty, Savvy." He closes his eye again. "But, fuck, why do you have to yell so goddamn early in the morning?"

"You're sweet talking is not getting you out of trouble, Matteo. You owe me a new bed." I walk out of the room, leaving him there to drown in whatever misery he's gotten himself into this go-around.

I didn't see any blood, no open wounds, so he's fine. The first time he turned up to my house with a bullet lodged in his thigh, I freaked out. I wanted to call his dad and demand answers as to why he'd let his fourteen year old son get shot. I was strongly advised not to yell at the infamous mafia Don by Matteo *and* his brother Theo, who had followed him to my house.

Their warnings should have been enough to stop me; they weren't. I dialed Matteo's father and yelled at him, told him exactly what I thought. Within minutes, a dozen blacked-out SUVs pulled up on my street and Matteo's dad was storming inside.

Even with a bullet embedded in his leg, Matteo jumped up and threw himself in front of me, preparing to fight his own father to keep me safe. He didn't need to though. Mr. Valentino just instructed all of us to get in the car, strongly advising us to *call him first next time*. He thanked me and said I'd make a better made man than anyone else he knew.

I don't think he realized just how afraid I was that night. Not for my own safety. No, I was terrified of losing Matteo. And that fear's never left me.

Even now, as I make coffee for the drunken idiot and contemplate how I'm going to make him pay for ruining yet another one of my mattresses, I wouldn't change a thing. I would rather him turn up at all hours of the night and sleep off his demons than be anywhere else. At least, when he's here, I don't have to wonder if he's still alive. I don't have to pray to God, asking him not to take my person.

Matteo walks into the kitchen and wraps an arm around my shoulders. I duck and pull away from him. "At least shower your whores off before you touch me with those hands of yours." I screw up my face.

Matteo smirks, grabbing the outstretched coffee mug I'm offering him. It takes everything I have not to ogle him, not to stare at his bare chest and abs, as he stands in my kitchen in nothing but a pair of slacks with the top button undone.

"So what I'm hearing, Savvy, is that if I go shower real quick, you'll let me touch you with these hands of mine? What would Dr. Jerk think of that?" He raises an eyebrow.

"Not likely. But if you shower, I'll let you stand in my kitchen a little longer. As for Dr. Jerk, he won't be coming around anymore." I open the refrigerator, not because I'm hungry but because I need to distract myself.

"Why? What'd he do?" he asks a little too casually, although there's a hint of his usual *I'll kill him if he hurt you* vibe in his tone.

"He didn't do anything. We just weren't compatible." I shrug. I can't exactly tell him that I broke it off with the hot doctor because the man just didn't light a candle to my best friend, that no one seems to be able to.

"You know you want me to touch you, Sav. Admit it. You know I can bring you all kinds of pleasure... the likes of which you've never seen before."

Shutting the fridge, I turn and glare at him. "Trust me, Matteo, I've seen it. I remember it, and it really wasn't that good." I walk out of the kitchen and head to my bedroom. I need to get ready for the day. I have to get to work.

"Come on, Sav, we were fucking fifteen. I've gotten a lot fucking better since then. I demand a do-over." Matteo stands in my doorway, leaning against the frame.

"Not happening. I gotta go to work, Matteo, and you need to—I don't know—do whatever it is you do during the day."

"It's not daytime yet, Savvy. It's still the middle of the fucking night. I'm going back to bed. Wake me up when you get home."

Before I can remind him that he has his own *home* and bed to go to, he's gone. And I hear the door to the guest room slam behind him.

2

MATTEO

He will win who knows when to fight and when not to fight.

— Sun Tzu, The Art of War

"Arrgh!" Really, again. My head pounds in rhythm with the banging currently sounding on my front door. I'm about to shoot whoever the fuck thinks knocking on my door at this hour of the morning is a good idea.

If I wanted to fucking talk to anyone, I'd be talking to them. Not trying to get some goddamn sleep. It's not until I pull myself up and out of bed that I look around and realize I'm not even in my own house. I'm at

Savvy's place. In her guest room and not her actual bed, unfortunately. A vague conversation about owing her a new mattress comes to mind, and as I look around, I can see why. There's an empty bottle of Jack beside me, its contents pooling in each of the divots in the pillow-top.

The banging on the door intensifies. "Fuck off!" I yell as I throw my shirt over my head, pick up my piece, and check that the chamber is loaded. I don't know who the fuck is banging on Savvy's door but they're about to get a *piece* of my goddamn mind.

My head aches. It feels like little jackhammers are digging into my brain as I make my way to the foyer. Without bothering to look through the peephole, I pull the door open and aim my pistol at the fucker standing with his fist raised midair, as if he's ready to knock again.

"What the fuck are you doing here?" I growl at my older brother. I don't lower my gun. I should. We both know I'm not going to fucking shoot him. *Maybe one in the shoulder would be okay though.* He wouldn't be able to pound on my fucking door with a slung arm.

"Put that away." Theo runs his eyes up and down my disheveled frame with a look of pure disgust on his face. "And put some fucking shoes on. We got work to do."

As much as I want to tell him to go and *fuck himself* and whatever jobs he deems more urgent than my much-needed sleep, I don't.

Why?

Because like Sun Tzu says: when you know when to fight and not fight, you'll always win. Judging by my brother's face right now, I know it's time to lower my weapon. Both literally and metaphorically.

My older brother's always been a tense bastard. I'm sure if you Googled the words *grouchy asshole,* you'd see a photo of Theo Valentino III right beside the definition.

Yep, you heard that right, *the third.* The first Theo Valentino was my grandfather (my dad's stepfather). I never met the man, but I've heard stories of the unforgiving, ruthless mafia Don. The second Theo Valentino is the current reigning boss of the Valentino family, AKA *Pops.* My old man. And, well, let's just say I'm his favorite son and even I wouldn't want to get on his bad side.

Then we have my eldest brother, Theo Junior— even though he's actually the third to carry the name— next in line for the throne so to speak. I forgive a lot of his assholeness for that reason. He has a lot to live up to when he takes over the family businesses. Definitely not a job I envy.

The way I see things, Theo's the heir and I'm the spare. And I'm fucking happy to avoid the title. Not once have I had my eye on the position my brother holds. If anything, I've pitied him for the path he's destined to walk. I might be the second son, but one day I know I'll be in Theo's current position, the underboss. However, that's still a long way from heading the entire family.

I get to have somewhat of a normal life. I was able to choose what I wanted to study in college. Theo didn't have that luxury; it was always going to be an MBA degree for him. As many illegitimate businesses and dealings we dabble in, we have just as many (if not more) legitimate businesses that need a competent CEO running them. That job falls to my father and Theo.

Once I've shoved my feet into my boots, I walk back out to find Theo looking around Savvy's living room. "Still haven't upgraded from the guest room, I see." He laughs.

"Fuck you," I growl. I don't bother giving him any other response as I stomp out the door. He knows that I plan to marry Savvy. I've always known she's the girl I'll spend the rest of my life with. And that life will begin just as soon as I can convince her of the same. Convince her we belong together. Something I'll be able to do the moment I finally get inside her head and figure out what her hold-ups about us are.

As well as we know each other, that is the one thing I've never been able to dissect.

I will marry her though. I'll make it my mission to ensure she's the happiest wife to have ever existed. It won't be anytime soon, but it'll happen. I feel it in my soul.

"WHAT ARE WE DOING HERE?" I ask, peering out the car window at the rundown warehouse. A warehouse I know all too well. It's the one we use when we're looking to get our hands dirty.

"Sammy Donaldson," Theo says, and the name alone tells me what I'm about to do.

"Fucking Sammy D, you couldn't have warned me? These are my fucking good jeans, Theo." I look down at my two-thousand-dollar pants, which are about to be covered in fucking blood before I have to burn them. Such a fucking waste of designer clothes.

"I'm sorry. Would you like me to wait so you can go and get yourself a mani-pedi too? Oh, and while you're there, might as well look for your fucking balls." Theo jumps out of the car.

"Asshole," I mutter under my breath before following him into the warehouse. "You know there's nothing wrong with taking care of yourself and looking good, Theo. You should try it sometime. Maybe then that cute little barista you're crushing on wouldn't be playing hard to get." I laugh, as I watch his face twist in both anger and frustration, and duck just before his hand comes out to slap me across the head.

My brother has been pining over a girl named Maddie who lives in Brooklyn. Do you have any idea how far fucking Brooklyn is? I do, because I've followed his ass there every night this week.

All thoughts stop when I enter the room currently housing Sammy D. He's chained up, his wrists in metal cuffs that are no doubt cutting into his skin as they support his weight. The rusty links that are slung over an old metal butcher's hook swing with his every movement. His toes just barely reaching the ground. By the looks of it, our boys have already given him a pretty decent once-over. His left eye is swollen shut, his bottom lip split open with drool hanging out of his mouth. Blood pours from a gash on the side of his head, the red-tinged liquid running down past his shoulder.

Whatever punishment Sammy D has already endured, he hasn't seen anything yet. There's a reason Theo brought me out here. Because my brother knows I'm the fucking best at what I do. This is where I fucking shine. I'm in my element when it comes to torturing information out of our enemies.

To the public eye, I'm Matteo Valentino, criminal defense attorney. I might be newly graduated, but when you're working for the family or friends of the family, it doesn't matter how many years of experience you have behind you. The only thing that matters is how well you can do your fucking job.

And why would a mafia prince become a defense attorney? Because every productive mafia family needs a good fucking lawyer who can bail their asses out of shit, am I right? I wasn't about to live my life, knowing that my father or any one of my brothers or friends could be locked up and I wouldn't be able to do a thing about it.

It was after I made my first kill at sixteen that I decided I was going to become a defense attorney. And when I've made my mind up about something, there's not much that will ever sway me. So I fucking studied my ass off, all through high school and all through college, to make sure I not only graduated and passed the bar, but also knew what I was fucking doing in a court room. While I might come across as the class clown, the one always down for a good time, that's not who I really am.

To my family, the ones who know me best, I'm Matteo Valentino, the merciless enforcer who can get blood out of a stone, so to speak. And right now, my job is to get this fucker, Sammy D, to give up his boss's location. Because the man calling the shots, Danny S, tried to fuck over *the* family. He owes us a large sum of money and is currently hiding underground, like the cockroach that he is. But the thing with hiding underground, with trying to outrun the Valentinos, is that there are only so many places you can be. So far you can run. And we'll always find you.

Danny S has been on the run for two weeks. He's outlasted most, but I can feel it—the fucker is running straight into a dead-end tunnel, and I'll be right fucking behind him. The only way out of this mess he's caused is in a goddamn body bag.

Reaching behind my head, I pull my shirt off—it

cost me a small fortune and I'm not about to get it messed up—and my brother raises a single eyebrow at me, shaking his head with the gesture.

"What? I thought I'd let Sammy D here get a glimpse of this work of art." I motion a hand up and down my torso. "It's the last thing he's going to see after all, and even a piece of shit like him deserves a glimpse of heaven before he finds himself in the pits of hell." I shrug.

"Right." Theo walks to the back of the room where two of our men, Rocco and Joey, are sitting at a makeshift table.

I look to the man in question, whose face visibly pales when he notices he now has my full attention. "Matteo, I don't know anything, man. This is a mistake," he pleads. They always plead; you'd think if you're in this line of work, you'd know that pleading or begging gets you fucking nowhere.

The thing about me that most people don't know until it's too late is that I don't have an ounce of mercy in me. I love hearing their pleas, love that they beg me to stop, beg me to let them go. Not once have I ever shown anyone the mercy they so desperately seek. Today is not going to be the day I start either.

"Hold that thought a minute, Sammy. I just remembered something I had to do," I tell him, pulling my phone from my pocket. I send a text to Amy; she runs a furniture store in the city. She and Theo had a thing once for about a week. She still holds out hope he'll figure out he's in love with her someday. I'm sure once she realizes that he's been struck down by the lovebug named Maddie, and that any chance she had is now long gone, she'll move on to someone else with the trust fund to support her dreams of becoming a trophy wife.

ME:

I need a king-sized bed delivered and assembled today.

I get a response right away, not that I had any doubt she'd reply instantly.

AMY:

Can you be more specific? What kind? Wood? Fabric? A color scheme at the very least?

ME:

Orange.

I smile. Savvy is not going to be impressed. And I may be the one begging for mercy when she's done with me after this. She says she hates orange. I call bullshit. I know exactly why she pretends to hate orange. It's the same reason I love the color. Because every time I see an orange-themed bedroom, I'm taken right back to when we were fumbling fifteen-year-old kids, losing our virginities to each other. I'm certain it takes her back to that night as well. Which is precisely why I'm choosing it.

I might be pushing it, but maybe it's time she started accepting that we're soul mates. That we're going to end up together.

3

SAVANNAH

Love prospers when a fault is forgiven, but dwelling on it separates close friends.

Proverbs 17:9

I'm going to kill him!

I really mean it this time. I'm going to wrap my hands around his neck and strangle the life out of him, smile while I watch him take his last breath. This is it. He's gone too far. How many times can you forgive someone who is supposed to be your best friend? How many times can I just turn a blind eye to his bullshit?

Staring at the monstrosity that is now in my guest

room, I dig my phone out of the bag that is still slung over my shoulder. I walked into my apartment two minutes ago, and for some reason, my feet brought me straight to this doorway. Something was telling me I had to look.

I can't believe he did this. He knows I hate orange. He knows I can't stand to look at the color. Because when I do, all I see is him. His naked body on top of mine as we gave ourselves to each other. All I see is a memory of something I want to experience again. Something I so desperately need but can't have.

And now my whole guest room is done up in a mixture of various shades of fucking orange. I dial his number. I know no matter what he's doing he'll answer. He always does. We made a pact, back when we were twelve, to never ignore each other's calls. This time is no different. I'm the only one who has ever broken that pact. Once. And I swore never to do it again.

"Savvy, not a good time, babe."

"Don't you *babe* me, Matteo John Valentino. Where are you?"

"Ah, I'm in Brooklyn. Why? What's wrong?"

"What's wrong? Seriously? What's wrong? I'm going to find you and gut you like a damn fish. I hate you, Matteo. You hear me? *Hate.* I want this shit out of my fucking house now!" I scream, hanging up the phone. It rings in my hand right away, and as much as I want to press ignore and decline his call, I can't. I answer it. "What?"

"Savvy, calm down. I have no idea what the hell you're talking about."

"Oh? So, if it wasn't you who just filled my guest room with every shade of orange there is in the goddamn rainbow, then who was it?"

"You told me to replace the bed and bedding, Savvy. That's what I did," he says.

"Why would you pick orange, Tao?" I use the nickname that only I ever get away with calling him. I like that I have my own little name for him.

"Why wouldn't I? The best time of my life was spent surrounded by orange."

I'm speechless. *How do I respond to that without showing all of my cards?* It's not like I can tell him that night was also the best night of my life. I can't admit that I regret running away from him. That I hate myself for not being able to just get over my own insecurities about him and let things progress naturally between us. How do I tell my best friend that I will never love another man like I love him, but I don't want him because I don't trust him with my heart?

It's not that I think he'd break it on purpose. I just don't think he'd have a choice. What he does, what his family does—well, there's not exactly a long lifespan for men like Matteo. I've accompanied him to way too many funerals already, and we're only in our twenties.

"I have to go," I say, running from my feelings, instead of facing them head-on like I should.

AN HOUR LATER, I've showered and changed into my comfy *I'm not leaving my couch* sweats and an old college shirt I stole from Matteo. A freshly opened bottle of sugary-sweet sparkling white wine sits in the ice bucket on the coffee table in front of me. Okay, it's already half empty, or maybe it's half full. Depends on how you look at it really. It probably wasn't the smartest idea to consume a good portion of the bottle in ten minutes, but I'm sure once the relaxing buzz kicks in, I'll be thinking it was the best idea since sliced bread.

The rest of the table is covered in my favorite snacks: chocolate, chocolate cookies, chocolate brownies. I think you catch my drift. My dinner tonight consists of chocolate and white wine. I'm covering at least two food groups here. Dairy (if you count the milk part of the chocolate) and fruit.

Christian Grey fills the huge flat screen on the wall —the over-the-top television Matteo insisted I needed. I sigh. Though, when I get a close-up of my favorite fictional character in those jeans, well, I have to say I agree with him. I do need a screen the size of a movie theatre. My mind drifts to the hunky, doting, *obsessed* billionaire.

Why can't I have one of those? Why hasn't anyone created a delivery app where I can get myself a Christian Grey dropped off on my doorstep?

Right as this thought flits through my mind, the sound of the doorbell rings out in my apartment. I look to the door but refuse to move from the couch. Whoever it is, I'm pretty damn sure it's not Christian, or any shades of Grey waiting for me on the other side.

The sound of a key being inserted in the lock has my head turning back to the noise and my eyes rolling. I wonder, if Matteo saw my expression, would he spank me?

Nope. Not even going there. That thought has no place in my head. It must be the wine talking. I turn my attention back to the movie, which I've watched so many times I can recite it line by line.

Don't look at him. Don't give him the satisfaction, I tell myself as I hear Matteo's footsteps leading into my living room.

"Shit, Savvy, I'm sorry." He sinks down into the seat next to me, and I do my best not to let the tears fall as he wraps his arm around my shoulders and pulls me into his side.

"What do you want, Tao?" I ask him.

"I got here as fast as I could. I didn't know you'd get this level of upset over my choice in bedding." He waves at the coffee table full of chocolate snacks.

"I'm not. I'm just hungry," I lie, pulling away from him. I don't miss the hurt that crosses over his features when I force distance between us. Why is he bothered? Why am I getting so many mixed signals from him? Am I that far gone that I'm now seeing things that just aren't there?

"*Fifty Shades*, wine, and chocolate. That's your recipe for: make me forget the world," he states.

"Not everything is about you, Matteo. Some things in my life have absolutely nothing to do with you. Shocking, I know."

"Really, like what? Because my whole world revolves around you, Savvy."

"Your whole world, huh? What about that family oath you took? How is that about me?" The minute the words are out of my mouth, I know I've fucked up. It's a sore subject between the two of us, and it's really not something I want to throw in his face like that. The Valentino family business is not something I want to be involved in. It's not something I want Matteo to be involved in. But it's also not something I'll ever get a say in. We both do our best to ignore that elephant.

I remember begging him about it when we were fifteen. I literally cried, pleading with him not to follow that path. I wanted him to choose differently for himself. He ended up telling me that he could never turn his back on his family. The thing I both love and hate about Matteo is his loyalty. He would never leave his family behind; he will always do whatever is necessary to protect them. No matter the cost.

And the costs are high. I've seen them. I was the one

holding him when the nightmares started. We were just sixteen. He didn't tell me what happened, but he didn't have to. I knew what he did, what he felt he had no choice to do. My best friend made his first of many kills before he was even legally considered an adult. I remember that night. His cousin Hope went missing, he found her, and let's just say things didn't end well for the boy who'd attacked her. Matteo had returned to my place in the middle of the night, a new kind of lost look in his eyes. I knew the minute I saw him that something bad had happened.

"We're not having this conversation right now, Savvy." Matteo drops his head into his hands, breaking me from the grasp of my memories.

"Let's go out," I blurt. It's Tuesday night. I don't know why I'm proposing this, but for some ungodly reason, I want to get away.

"What?"

"Come on, I want to go dancing." I jump up from the couch. Yes, dancing suddenly seems like the best idea I've had this decade.

"In that?" He looks me up and down.

"Give me two minutes." I run into my bedroom and pull my sweatshirt over my head and my sweatpants down my legs. I grab a little black dress from the hanger and slide it on. Removing the scrunchie that was holding my hair up in a messy pile, I tip my head upside down and ruffle my fingers through the knotted locks before snapping my neck back upright.

Then I grab a pair of black pumps and walk out to the living room. Matteo is standing by the stereo system pressing buttons. "House Party" by Sam Hunt starts blasting through the speakers. Matteo turns around. His eyes heat as they travel up and down the length of me, not once but twice. "Una fottuta bellezza senza sforzo," he says. *Effortless fucking beauty.*

I roll my eyes. I'm more than aware that I look a hot mess. I could be wearing a potato sack and Matteo would still tell me I'm *effortlessly beautiful.* I remember the first time he used that phrase. We were twelve and I teased him about reading the dictionary to come up with such a big word.

"We're not going out. We're dancing right here." He smirks.

"Here?" I look around my apartment.

"Yep," he says, and then starts singing along to the lyrics as he takes hold of my hand and spins me around.

A smile instantly lights up my face. I don't know where Matteo found this playlist; he probably created it himself. But the song that follows has us both singing (well, screaming really) from the top of our lungs. "Best Friend" by Saweetie is our jam. It's absolutely ridiculous, but ever since it came out, we yell the words as loud as we can at each other. By the time it's over, I'm puffing and out of breath, Matteo not so much.

"Thank you," I tell him. "I needed that."

"I know." He smiles a smile that makes my heart

skip a beat when "Issues" by Julia Michaels cues up next.

"Yeah, we do." I laugh when he sings the chorus. I ignore the part about him needing me. When the song finishes, I go and flick the music off. "I need a drink and you need to maybe find a vocal coach if you're going to keep belting out like that in my apartment."

He falls onto the sofa dramatically with a hand to his chest. "I'm hurt, babe. I thought you loved my singing."

"You thought wrong." I shake my head and fill my wine glass. I sit next to him. "Wanna watch the rest of the movie with me?"

"You know once, just once, I'd like to pick the fucking movie. You always get to choose, Savvy."

"Hey, this was already on when you barged in here, so you're either staying and watching it. Or, you know, you can go home *to your own place.*"

"If you moved in with me, we wouldn't have to keep two places," he says.

"I'm not moving in with you." I hit play on the movie, effectively ending the conversation we've had a million times before.

4

MATTEO

All warfare is based on deception.

— Sun Tzu, The Art of War

It's been two days since I've seen Savvy. I tucked her into bed after she fell asleep on the sofa halfway through the movie the other night. I thought about staying in her guest room again but decided to go home. I needed a breather before I did something I'd regret, like climbing into bed with her.

Pressing a button on the treadmill, I increase my speed. Working out my frustrations in the gym is better than the alternative: going and finding some fucking loser to fuck up. That's still on the cards though. Surely there's some idiot around dumb enough to owe the family a debt.

I may not have seen her, but our message thread over the last two days could probably fill a novel. I don't recall a day where we haven't spoken to each other, either in person, on the phone, or through text messages. Ever.

Sweat drips down my face as I run at a punishing speed. I need more. I want more. I reach out, upping my pace. Working out is something that usually eases the built-up tension I get whenever thoughts of Savvy invade my mind more than they should. I've been fucking patient. I've been waiting for her to wake up and realize that what we have is not something she'll ever find with anyone else.

Ten years I've waited. I may not have been a saint. I've fucked around plenty. But I've never dated anyone, never gone back to the same woman more than once. And not for a lack of effort on the woman's part. Many of them have tried to outstay their welcome in my bed. I don't have anything else to give them, other than one really epic fuck. Because everything else I have belongs to her. To Savvy.

Even if she won't admit that she wants what it is I have to give her. I'll keep waiting as long as it takes. Either that or I'll actually go fucking insane and do something irrefutably stupid.

I lift my shirt to wipe the sweat out of my eyes. My legs burn with each forceful thump on the rapidly cycling belt. I don't stop though. I push myself harder, faster. When I drop my shirt back down, my gaze connects with a pair of dark eyes that match my own. My father stands in front of the treadmill with a scowl that I swear is a permanent feature on his face.

Great, just how I wanted my day to start. Dealing with whatever shit he needs done. His hands are in the pockets of his pants. He's waiting.

Tugging the earbud from my ears, I hit the stop button on the machine, the belt slowing before it comes to a definitive stop. Then I pick up the towel I dropped on the floor and wipe my face and neck. "Pops, you're a little overdressed to work out." I give him that smart-ass grin of mine I know he loves to hate.

"Get dressed. You've got work to do," he says in reply.

"What work?" I ask. "I need a dress code, Pops. Last week Theo made me ruin a perfectly good pair of designer jeans."

He rolls his eyes and looks upwards, like he's seeking answers from above. "Matteo, I gave you your fucking trust fund. I also pay your salary. I know you can afford to replace the fucking jeans. Now get dressed and meet me outside in ten minutes." He walks out, slamming the door before I can try to annoy him into leaving me behind.

JUST BECAUSE I'M AN ASS, I slide into the back of my father's blacked-out Escalade exactly eleven minutes after he walked out of my home gym. He makes a point to look at his watch but he doesn't say anything about my one-minute tardiness.

"Where are we going anyway?" I ask.

"The courthouse. Romeo got arrested last night."

"And he's still there? What the fuck did he get taken in for? And why the fuck have they kept him this long?" I yell.

"Calm down. He's fine. I told George to make sure his bail hearing was set for this morning. A night in a cell might do the little shit some good."

"What'd he do?"

"Drunk and disorderly. He didn't have any ID on him, and the badge who brought him in didn't seem to care who he was when he started spewing out threats using the Valentino name."

Drunk and disorderly, that's easy. I really don't even need to be here. Romeo's smarter than all of us put together. Fuck, my brother could represent himself and be out before the gavel hit the sound block. What worries me is the fact he was drunk. That's not like him. His twin? Sure. Luca's fucking reckless as hell. But Romeo is more calculating, always wanting to be thinking straight. Sometimes I wonder if the kid's actually a robot, with the way he analyses everything and comes across as cold as fucking ice. Nothing usually fazes him at all.

§&

IT TOOK ALL of ten minutes to have Romeo out of the courthouse, released with nothing more than a slap on the wrist. He sits next to me in one of the Escalades currently delivering us to our parents' house. Dad's riding in another car; he purposely hasn't said a word to Romeo. The silent treatment from that man is worse than any amount of yelling and cursing he dishes out. It's when he doesn't say anything that you know you've really pissed him off.

Romeo rests his head back on the seat, his eyes closed. "How was jail?" I ask him.

Opening one eye, he somehow manages to scowl at me. "I've slept in nicer places," he grunts.

"You're a fucking trust fund brat. Of course you've slept in nicer places. Care to tell me what made you drink yourself stupid?" I pin him with the best glare I can muster up.

"Not particularly," he says, closing his eyes again.

"Well, it's either me or Pops. Or worse, Theo. So come on out with it. I can't help you if you don't tell me what the fuck had you trying to drink your problems away."

"You wouldn't understand."

"Try me."

Romeo rolls his eyes and huffs out a breath. "There's this girl..." he grinds his words between his teeth.

"There's always a girl." I laugh.

"Forget I said anything." He shuts down again.

"Come on, what about the girl?"

"I like her a little too fucking much. That's never happened before."

"You drank yourself stupid, put yourself in a fucking vulnerable position, because you like a girl?" I ask.

"Told you, you wouldn't understand."

"Yeah, because I haven't been in love with the same girl since I was fucking six." It's no secret to my family how much Savannah means to me.

"How is Savvy?" Romeo asks, in an attempt to change the subject, a smirk splitting his face.

"Nice try. We're not finished. Does this girl have a name?"

"She does, but you're not getting it. I don't need you and Theo running your little checks and shit. She's fucking pure, innocent. Way too fucking good for our family."

"If you like her, then tell her."

"Yeah, that's not going to happen," he groans.

"Why not?"

"Didn't you hear me? She's too fucking innocent for our family."

I'm about to respond, give him plenty of reasons why he shouldn't run away from someone he likes just because of our family, when my cell starts blaring out the tone to "Best Friend," reminding me of just how much our last name impacts our relationships or would-be relationships. Retrieving my phone from my pocket, I hit answer. "Savvy, to what do I owe the pleasure?"

"Odd choice of words, seeing as you owe me five grand," she says in greeting.

"What for? Babe, if you need money, all you have to do is ask." I'd give her the whole world if she asked for it.

"I don't need your money, Tao. I bought your gift for Hunter and Julie's wedding this weekend, and you have really expensive taste." I can hear her smirk through the receiver.

"This weekend?"

"I knew you'd forget. You are not cancelling on me, Matteo. We're going to Vegas. You promised me you'd make it."

"I didn't forget. I just wanted to hear how much you were looking forward to spending a weekend in Vegas with me," I lie, because I totally fucking forgot. "I've got the jet already scheduled. I'll pick you up at six a.m."

"Thanks. Can't wait," she says. "What are you doing now?"

"Heading to my parents' place. Romeo seems to be living up to his namesake and is making stupid fucking decisions in the name of love." I laugh.

"It's not love," he grunts.

"Yeah, well, we all do stupid shit for those we love," Savvy replies.

"Like buy over-the-top wedding gifts for people who are nothing more than acquaintances."

"They've been our friends since middle school, Tao. I think they're plenty more than acquaintances."

"No, you're my friend. They're acquaintances. Besides, I don't need any more friends when I found the best one a guy could have."

"Smooth." Savvy laughs. "Don't be late. I gotta go."

"I won't be late," I tell her, hanging up just as we pull into the driveway of our parents' estate.

The moment we exit the car, Romeo turns to me. "Don't repeat what I told you," he pleads.

"Sure, but just so you know, I think any girl would be fucking lucky to have you, regardless of what your last name might be." I mean that too. My brother is loyal, trustworthy, and if he actually has feelings for this girl, he'll go above and beyond for her. I know him. The kid might like to act like he doesn't care, but he does.

As soon as we enter the house, we're greeted by the very disappointed glare of our mother.

"Okay, I'm out. I've done my part. This is all you, bro," I tell Romeo, slapping him on the shoulder.

"Don't you bloody move. You'll be next," Mom points a finger in my direction, halting me in my tracks.

"What'd I do?" I ask, holding a hand to my chest in genuine shock. I don't know why I'm in trouble too.

"Romeo, care to explain why you were out, by yourself. Drunk enough to get arrested?" She folds her arms over her chest. Oh, she's mad.

"I'm in college, Ma. Getting wasted is what college kids do." He does his best to play it off like it's not a big deal.

"Maybe, but you're not like most college kids, Romeo. You can't let your guard down like that. What if…." Mom lets her sentence trail off.

"I'm fine, Ma. Nothing happened." He wraps his arms around her and kisses her cheek.

"But it could have," she whispers.

I get it. He was out on his own. We have enough enemies, plenty of people wanting to take what's ours. He shouldn't ever be off like that. Drunk. Without backup.

"I won't do it again," he promises.

"Good. Now, your father wants to see you in his office." She steels her spine.

"Great. Looking forward to it." Romeo's shoulders straighten as I watch him make his way down the hall. I've always wondered what he'd do after college. Luca, we all know is going to end up in the NFL. But Romeo, he's fucking smart. He can be anything he wants to be.

"Now, it's your turn. Follow me." Mom turns and walks in the opposite direction of my father's office.

"Why am I in trouble? I haven't done anything?" Or at least not anything I'd ever admit.

"Do you need to be in trouble to have a cup of

coffee with your mother, Matteo?" She turns and smiles at me as we enter the kitchen.

"No, of course not," I say, sitting at the counter. Mom is silent as she busies herself making us both a cup of coffee.

"So, how are things?" she asks, handing me over my favorite mug. It's the one I got during a trip to Disneyland when we were kids.

"Fine." I watch her as I sip from the cup. She wants something, or is up to something. I don't know what but I know my mother. And when she wants something, she always gets it.

"Aunt Reilly called last night."

"How is she?" I question. My Aunt Reilly is my mom's identical twin sister, who stayed back in Australia when my mother moved to the city.

"You know, as erratic as always," Mom says. "Anyway, she mentioned how Chase and Hope are spending a few months in Melbourne, working on one of the Merge clubs there."

Hope is my cousin, one half of another set in a long line of twins that runs in our family. Her sister Lily is married to Sydney's underground crime boss, AKA Alex Mancini. "Hope's going to live in Melbourne by herself?" I question. I have always had a soft spot for my cousin. My first kill was for her. Because of her. Theo and I tracked her down when she snuck out one night. She was just sixteen, and she was being sexually attacked by some punk-ass kid who was supposed to be her boyfriend. I didn't even flinch as I pulled the trigger. If I could bring that asshole back from the dead, I would, just so I could kill him all over again.

"She's going with Chase, her husband, Matteo. She won't be alone." Mom laughs.

"Well, gee, that's comforting." I roll my eyes. I'm not a huge fan of the guy. Yes, he makes my cousin happy but that fucker is way too cocky for his own good. "I was discussing a trip Down Under with Theo the other day. I'm heading to Melbourne after Christmas actually. Perfect timing." I chug the rest of my coffee, standing before placing my cup in the sink.

"What are you going to Australia for?" Mom asks.

"Business. There's a lawyer there who asked me to assist him on a case." I hate deceiving my mother, but sometimes it's easier this way. I can't tell her that I'm going solely to be there for Hope. She'll have Pops force me to stay.

"Right," Mom replies, not believing a word I've just said.

"Is Savannah joining us for Christmas?"

"She always does. I gotta go. Thanks for the coffee." I lean down and kiss her cheek before making a hasty escape. I don't need another interrogation about the state of my and Savvy's relationship. My mother has been planning our wedding since we were six. Little does she know, I've also been planning that day. It'll happen, just as soon as I can get Savvy on board with the idea.

Jumping in the back of one of our cars, I pull out my phone and send a text.

ME:

> Since we'll be in Vegas, should I bring our marriage license? We can get hitched by Elvis.

SAVVY

Two are better than one, because they have a good return for their labor: If either of them falls down, one can help the other up. But pity anyone who falls and has no one to help them up. Also, if two lie down together, they will keep warm. But how can one keep warm alone?

Ecclesiastes 4:9-11

I look at the text message again and again. This isn't the first time he's joked about running away to Vegas to get married. It's just the first time I'm actually considering saying: *fuck it, why the hell not?*

I stare at my phone screen.

MATTEO:

> Since we'll be in Vegas, should I bring our marriage license? We can get hitched by Elvis.

Shaking my head, I remember all the reasons we shouldn't. The glaring one being that he's in the fucking mafia. And not just as a participant. He's a goddamn mafia prince. And, yes, I realize I've said the word *mafia* over and over. But sometimes I need to repeat it, to remind me what's at stake if I give in. I can't bear the pain of letting myself have him like that, to make him really mine and then have him ripped away. Because a bullet didn't just graze him this next time—it went straight through his head. Sure, it'll still destroy me if that happened now. But I've protected my heart a little by not fully giving into it. Or at least that's what I keep telling myself.

Curiosity gets the better of me. Does he actually have a marriage license? Though, knowing Matteo, I wouldn't put it past him.

ME:

> Since when do we have a marriage license? Also, I'm never getting married by an Elvis impersonator.

His response comes in immediately.

MATTEO:

> Since I got one a few years ago, which I keep updating every sixty days because what's life without hope, right? And that wasn't a no to my proposal.

ME:

> That wasn't a proposal either, and it's a no. We are not getting married! I'll see you in the morning. Don't be late.

MATTEO:

> Never say never, babe. See you in the morning.

NEVER SAY NEVER. Again I'm left confused as hell. Is he serious? Does he think we're going to end up together?

I'll keep to my *never going to happen* motto. Sometimes you have to say never. It's better for both of us if I keep saying it.

A knock at my open office door has me looking up. Kirstin, my personal assistant, pops her head in. "Morning, did you oversleep?" she asks, referring to the fact I was later than usual this morning.

"No, last-minute wedding gift shopping." I wave to the two separate Tiffany and Co. bags sitting on my sofa.

"Remind me to make sure you're the first person I invite to my wedding, and I expect two gifts too." She laughs.

"One is from me; the other is from Matteo."

"Speaking of that fine specimen, how is he?" Kirstin has never hidden the fact that she sees Matteo as a slice of hunky man-meat that should be savored. It would annoy me if she was actually into men and not settled down with her live-in girlfriend, Sienna.

"Annoying. What's on the schedule for today?" I ask, changing the subject.

"Ah, I rescheduled your nine thirty with Goodwin and Cobalt to eleven. They weren't impressed. Then you have an appointment at two with a new client, Loch Nielson. He's just purchased a penthouse that's completely empty. A whole blank canvas."

I should be thrilled. It's an interior designer's wet dream. But, this close to the holidays, all I feel is dread. That's going to be hours upon hours of work when all I want to do is go on vacation. "Great, thank you."

"Anytime, boss. It is what you pay for after all." Kirstin walks back out to her desk.

Checking the time, I note that it's eleven now. I groan with the realization, pick up my plans for Goodwin and Cobalt, and grab my bag and keys. I guess the quiet morning I was hoping for has gone out the window.

It's eight o'clock by the time I make it through the door of my apartment again. Dropping my bag on the entrance counter, I strip my blouse off as I make my way to the bathroom. A hot shower, comfy pjs, and chilled wine are in order after this day of hell.

I literally just spent the last five hours with Loch Nielson. A young app developer who recently hit it big time. The kid has absolutely no style, unless you count the obvious new money spending a *style* of its own. Which I do not. He wants everything to flash *I'm rich*, right down to the custom sofas and theatre system he claims are *must haves*.

Turning the shower on, I let the steam fill the room as I remove the remaining items of clothing from my body before jumping under the scalding water. I let my back rest against the cold tiles and slide to the shower floor. This is what I needed, a hot shower to wash the day away.

Half an hour later, my fingers are wrinkly and I find myself yawning. I still need to pack for the weekend, so I force myself out of this heavenly sanctuary. I throw on my robe and head into the guest room, cursing Matteo (again) when I'm assaulted by that god-awful color as soon as I open the door. Ignoring the theme of the room, I slip into the closet and retrieve my Louis Vuitton luggage before rushing out and slamming the door behind me.

An hour and three glasses of wine later, and I'm finally packed. I pile my bags in the foyer, then climb into bed. As I lie here, staring into the darkness, I mentally go through my to-do list. I get anxious when I have to go away, even if it's just for a weekend. I always have that feeling like I'm forgetting something. I'm pretty sure I've done everything I was supposed to do.

Gifts purchased. Check.

Hotel booked. Check.

The jet was Matteo's only task, and I'm sure he managed to do that. Or at least I hope he did—he said he did. So I let myself relax. I've got this. Everything will be fine.

§

HE'S LATE. Of course he's freaking late. It's Matteo freaking Valentino. Knowing him, he's passed out drunk after whatever shenanigans he got up to last night.

It's six thirty. I've been waiting, biting my nails, forcing myself not to call him. But enough is enough. He promised he'd be here on time. I'm not sure why I'm surprised. This isn't any different from the norm. The guy doesn't know the meaning of the phrase *on time*.

He picked me up for prom an hour after the dance had already started. He claimed he wanted us to make an entrance. The thing is, whatever room Matteo walks into, heads turn, eyes widen. He's always made an entrance without even trying.

Picking up my phone, keys, and luggage, I head down to my car. I should just call and wake him up, but what's the fun in that? If he can't just swing by, like he agreed, then I'll go and remind him. In person. I am not going to this wedding alone. I will drag him kicking and screaming if I have to.

It takes me ten minutes to pull into Matteo's garage. We live only a few blocks from each other, which is why I've never understood how he always seems to end up in my guest bedroom. Swiping my thumb on the button, I take the elevator right up to his penthouse. There's two beefy guys sitting in his foyer. I've seen Matteo's shadows—as I like to call them—all my life. Yet they still give me the creeps. Ignoring his men, I head straight to his room, with a quick detour to the kitchen to get a glass of cold water.

I take a deep breath, preparing myself. I really do not want to walk in on him and another woman. That's never actually happened, but there's always a first time for everything, right? Thankfully he's alone when I enter his bedroom. However, he's naked, lying on his stomach, with the bedsheet covering only half of his ass. I stand there. Hovering. My fingers itch to pull the thin material the rest of the way down, because Matteo's ass is a sight to behold. His back is all muscle. I want to run my tongue, my hands, all over it.

Nope, this is not happening. I am not thinking illicit thoughts about my best friend right now. Lifting the glass of water, I pour it over his head. Even if I'm the one who needs to cool down.

"Ah, what the…" Matteo rolls over, but it's not the

gun in his hand that has me stunned and frozen to the spot. It's the fact that he's naked and now giving me an eyeful of his cock. And what a nice freaking cock it is. I can't bring myself to look away. I know I've seen it before, but that was a really long time ago. "Savvy, what the hell? Are you trying to get yourself fucking shot?" he grunts, throwing the firearm down on the bed. I stand there, rooted to my spot, still staring at a part of my best friend I really shouldn't be. "Like what you see, babe? You can touch it if you want. He won't bite." Matteo grabs his cock and gives it a slow pump.

This breaks me out of my stupor. Because that's all it was. Shock. I do not want to wrap my mouth around my best friend's cock. I do not want to taste him. Nope, not even a little. "I've seen better. Get up and get dressed. You were late." I somehow manage to walk out of the room without taking a second look at him—or certain parts of his anatomy. It was a damn struggle though.

By the time Matteo appears in the kitchen, I have two travel cups full of coffee, one with vanilla creamer for me, the other straight black for him. "Before you say anything, it wasn't my fault. My alarm didn't go off." He wraps an arm around my shoulder and pulls me into his chest. "I'm sorry."

"I'm buying you ten alarm clocks for Christmas, Tao," I tell him, sinking into his embrace momentarily before I pull away. I'm always the first to pull away. The fact that Matteo never ends our hugs does not escape my notice. Though it does confuse me. Because lately my mind is a jumbled mess when it comes to my best friend's feelings for me. "Here, coffee. Please, for the love of all that is holy, tell me you actually have the jet ready," I plead, handing over his bitter black coffee.

"Of course, I do. Come on. Did you drive here?" he asks, placing a hand on my lower back.

"No, I flapped my arms and flew." I roll my eyes at his ridiculous question.

"Sassy Savvy's in the house today! I love it."

We walk into the foyer, where Matteo stops and says something to his men in rapid Italian. I've picked up a few key words over the years, but when he speaks quickly, I have no idea what he's saying. He knows this, which is why he does it. I think it's because he realizes I don't really want to be involved in his business dealings so he spares me from having to hear any of it.

"Sure, boss," one of the men says in response to whatever Matteo has told or requested of them. I might not be able to understand what Matteo's saying, but that doesn't stop the tingling in my nether regions. My panties dampen. There is just something inherently sexy about the Italian language.

"Let's hit the road. You can drive." Matteo grabs the prepacked bag sitting by the elevator doors.

We settle onto the road in a comfortable silence. Music plays low on the radio as I keep stealing glances of Matteo every now and then, but do my best to keep my eyes focused in front of me. The airport is forty-five minutes away. We still have twenty minutes to go until we reach it. Matteo has been furiously typing on his phone. I don't bother asking who or what he's texting about. I doubt I want to know the answer anyway. He finally pockets his phone and turns to look at me—*stares* would be a better word.

Ignore him, Savvy. Ignore.

After a couple of minutes beneath his heated gaze, I break. "What?" I turn and ask him.

"Just admiring your beauty, babe." He winks.

I feel the blush creep up my neck. I roll my eyes and return my attention to the road. "Admit it. You totally forgot about this weekend, didn't you?" I laugh, changing the subject.

"I'm spending a weekend in Vegas with my best friend. How could I possibly forget about that?"

"Uh-huh. Sure."

"You did book the hotel, didn't you?" he asks.

"Yes. Because unlike you, I'm a perfectly functioning, responsible adult."

YOU KNOW what they say about famous last words and all. Well, that thought pops into my head as I do my best not to lose my cool with the young clerk in front of me. "What do you mean you don't have my reservation?" I practically scream in the guy's face at the Bellagio. Okay, I said I was trying not to lose my cool, not that I'd be successful at it.

"I'm sorry, ma'am. There was a double booking. Your reservation has been fully refunded," he says, like I should just be happy with that.

"I don't care about the refund. I need that room," I screech.

"We're fully booked. Sorry. Maybe try another hotel." The arrogant prick smiles at me.

Matteo has been silent the whole time I've been arguing with this dipshit. He knows I don't want or need him to come to my defense. He's tried it a few times in the past and has ended up being the one on the other end of my wrath. I look over to him. I'm about to blow my gasket. I open my mouth to spew a barrage of insults when Matteo shakes his head at me.

He pulls out his wallet, hands over a credit card, and glares at the guy. "I'm sure there is a room somewhere in this hotel for us." His voice is firm, assured.

The clerk shakes his head. "I'm sorry, Mister..." He glances down at the card in his hand, and I see it. The moment he realizes who he's talking to. "Ah, Valentino. Mr. Valentino. Of course, sir, I can get you into the penthouse suite," he says as he starts typing away on the keyboard. "On the house, obviously."

"That would be great. Thank you." Matteo smiles at me.

I don't smile back. *How the hell does this man's name get him everything he wants?*

Fear. That's how. Everyone in their right mind fears the Valentino crime family. I hate that he had to use his pull to get us a room.

If the penthouse was available, why the hell didn't the clerk offer it to me? Do I look like I can't afford it?

Asshole.

Matteo grabs the key from the clerk, who is apologizing to him. *Profusely.* I turn and follow Matteo, when he stops abruptly, looking back at the guy at the desk. "Anything she wants this weekend, I expect you to make sure she fucking gets it."

I sink into myself. I don't like the attention. Everyone is looking at us. Staring.

"Come on, babe, this is going to be the best weekend ever." Matteo takes my hand and leads me to the elevator. Once we're closed safely inside, he turns to me. "So, you had the hotel booked, huh?"

"I did," I say between clenched teeth.

"It's fine. Don't get so worked up over it. Now we have the best room here."

The doors to the luxurious penthouse open and we enter into a small foyer that leads to an open living space. White sofas trimmed in gold sit in the center, facing a huge flat-screen television hanging above a fireplace. There's a little kitchen off to the side, the countertop lined with dark-green leather stools. I kick off my shoes and my feet sink into the plush carpet. This room is nice, probably a lot nicer than the double room I had originally booked.

Leaving Matteo in the living area, I walk down the hall. The first door leads to a bedroom with a huge oversized bed filled to the brim with plush pillows. There's another door opposite it and I thank my lucky stars that there are two bedrooms here. And my smile falls the moment I turn the knob. It's not a bedroom; it's an office. Who the hell needs an office in a hotel suite? This cannot be happening to me. Please, God, I can't handle this. One bed plus one sinfully hot best friend equals…

Nope, this is not going to be one of those situations. It will be one bed plus one sinfully hot best friend sleeping on the sofa.

"Matteo!" I yell at the top of my lungs.

6

MATTEO

Victorious warriors win first and then go to war, while defeated warriors go to war first and then seek to win.

— Sun Tzu, The Art of War

I run down the hall at the sound of Savvy's scream, my heart pounding and a cold sweat beginning to break out across my skin. I'm expecting the worst. When I reach her, I shove her behind my back and enter the room she was staring into.

It's an office. An empty fucking office. I spin around to find her with her arms folded against her chest.

"Why the hell are you screaming bloody murder? There's nothing fucking here, Savvy."

"Exactly. *That* should be a bedroom, Tao. It's an office! I hope you like sleeping on a desk, because I'm taking the bedroom." She pivots and stomps across the hall.

I reach the door just as she attempts to slam it shut. Pushing past her, I look at the bed. "It's big enough. We can share it," I tell her, sitting on the end of the mattress.

"Uh, no, we can't." Her eyes widen at my suggestion.

"Why not? We've shared a bed plenty of times, Savvy."

"When we were kids. We haven't shared a bed since..." She lets her sentence trail off.

I look to the heavens for patience. "Savannah, your virtue is safe with me. I promise I'll keep my hands to myself and stay on my side of the bed."

"You already took my virtue, Matteo. And besides, it's not just your hands I'm worried about. What if I have a dream or something and think you're Rip Wheeler?"

"Who the fuck is Rip Wheeler?" I grunt and push to my feet.

"From *Yellowstone*. Do you not listen to anything I talk about?"

"He's a fictional character? Babe, if you want to play out your cowboy fantasies on me, I'm not going to stop you."

"Shut up."

"It'll be fine. You won't even notice I'm there," I tell her as I walk past to exit the room. *I* sure as hell will notice *she's* fucking there. I doubt I'll get a wink of fucking sleep this weekend. My balls are going to be the new picture next to the term *blue balls* in the Urban Dictionary.

Heading straight to the wet bar, I pour myself a drink. I'm going to need a lot of alcohol this weekend. Maybe if I give myself a case of whiskey dick, it won't be so hard sleeping next to Savvy.

Pun intended.

Who am I kidding? Not even whiskey can keep my dick from wanting that girl. It's been wanting to get back inside her since we were fifteen.

"Can you pour me one of those?" Savvy's voice fills the otherwise silent living room.

"Sure you can handle being close enough to me to come and get it?" I don't turn around. I don't look at her. I do, however, pour her a drink.

"I'm sorry. You're right. It's fine to share a bed. I just… I don't want to ruin this, Matteo. You're all I have and I don't want to do anything that will jeopardize our friendship," she says.

"You're wrong, you know," I tell her, pivoting on my heel and holding out the glass to her.

"About what?"

"First, that I'm all you have. You have my whole family, Savvy. You know they'd do anything for you.

You are one of us. And, second, that there is anything in this world you could possibly do that would ruin what we have. Nothing, and I mean nothing, will ever come between us, Savvy. I won't let it."

"I know you think that, Tao, but not even you can stop the Armageddon."

"I don't know… I'd go down trying though." I would fall on any sword for Savvy; she knows it. My phone starts vibrating in my pocket. "Hold that thought." Raising a finger, I stop whatever reply Savvy had on the tip of her tongue as I retrieve my cell. "Theo, one sec," I answer my brother's call, then place my palm over the speaker. "Go and get ready. We're hitting the town tonight, babe."

She smiles wide as she nods her head and runs back down the hallway. Savvy loves to go out dancing.

"Okay, shoot. Well, not literally. Unless you are about to pull the trigger and it's not aimed at me, then go ahead," I say into the receiver of my phone.

"I don't even know where to start with that. Are you high?" Theo asks me.

"On life, yes," I deadpan. We don't touch drugs. That's a cardinal family sin. Drink yourself into a coma, no problem. But start taking drugs and, well, that's when you'll find yourself with a new pair of cement shoes, taking up residency in the East River. In a manner of speaking.

"I've got a job for you to do while you're in Vegas.

I've sent Rocco and Joey. They'll be meeting you tomorrow morning first thing," he tells me.

"You do know I'm here to attend a friend's wedding, right? I'm pretty sure even the Pope gets a day off every decade."

"Don't compare yourself to the Pope, Matteo. You wouldn't last a minute in that man's shoes. Also, I wasn't aware Savannah was getting married."

"She's not," I growl.

"Well then, you're not there for a friend's wedding, now, are you? She's the only friend you have, fucker." He laughs.

"Okay, an acquaintance then. It doesn't matter. I'm here to attend a wedding and I'm not explaining to Savvy why I can't go with her."

"Yeah, me neither." I hear him inhale as I'm sure he attempts to not lose his shit. "You'll make it to the wedding, Matteo. Just meet with the guys tomorrow. I'm sending you a location."

"Fine. What am I doing anyway?" I ask. With my family, it could be anything from having tea with the King of England, to taking his throne by force.

"Putting that hundred-thousand-dollar degree to use. Someone is in need of some legal advice."

"What kind of legal advice? What's the case?"

"RICO charges," he says.

"Well, fuck, I'm glad it's nothing serious like a DUI. Damn, RICO? Who the fuck am I supposed to be doing the damn near impossible for?"

"Tony Gambino."

Tony Gambino, the head of one of the Las Vegas outfits. I've heard of him. I'm surprised he let himself get caught. Legend has it he's one of the most intelligent men the criminal underworld has ever seen. "Surely they have their own in-house counsel," I argue.

"He does. But he requested you and we owe him a favor. Once you're done, our debt is settled, and he'll owe us so much more."

"Fine. Send me the details." I hang up and refill my glass. Some getaway weekend this has turned out to be.

"ONE MORE…" Savvy slurs into my ear as she leans her whole weight against me. I should stop her. I've been making her drink a shit-ton of water between cocktails. She pouts those bright red lips of hers, her blonde curls fall into her face, and she blows at them in vain, trying to get them off her sweat-drenched skin.

We've been dancing, drinking, and then dancing some more. For six hours. It's now two a.m. and I know if I don't drag her to bed soon, she's going to curse me out in the morning. We've both had our fair share of drinks. I stopped a while back, though, when I saw how wasted she planned on getting. I reach up and tuck the stray strands behind her ear.

"Please, Tao. Pretty, pretty please with a cherry on top." Great, now she's batting those damn lashes at me.

Well, trying to anyway. It looks more like she's attempting to take flight, but the woman is still damn irresistible.

I've never been able to tell her no. "One more and then we're leaving," I say into her ear.

Her hands grab both sides of my face, and the next thing I know, her lips are on mine. It's only for a moment, but I'm frozen to the spot, my eyes wide. Savvy pulls back and smiles. "I love you, Matteo Valentino. How'd I get so lucky as to have you as my best friend?"

There's that word again. *Friend.* I've never loathed and loved a word so much in my life. "I think we both know I'm the lucky one here, babe," I tell her.

"Nope, I'm definitely lucky." She leans over the counter, signaling for the bartender. I push off my stool and stand directly behind her, covering the view of her ass she was granting the whole damn bar. She's wearing a black glittery scrap of material. She claims it's a dress but I've seen bigger fucking pocket squares.

The bartender comes over. I'll give him credit though. His eyes don't stray down to the cleavage popping out of the top of her dress. Once she has her drink in hand, Savvy spins around, stumbles, and drops the whole glass on the ground. The bright-blue contents cover both of us.

"Okay, I think that's it. Let's go." I press her body to mine and start walking out of the club.

"No, one more dance, Tao. Just one more," she pleads, struggling against my hold.

"We'll find somewhere else to dance, babe," I tell her with no intention of following through.

"Okay."

Once we're out on the street, I put her down and pull her close, wrapping my arm around her waist as we begin the three-block walk back to the Bellagio.

7

SAVVY

Do to others as you would have them do to you.

Luke 6:31

$\mathcal{I}$ feel like a thousand little ninjas are practicing their karate kicks on the inner lining of my brain. "Make it stop," I groan, rolling over and curling into the plush duvet, my movements stopping when I hit a wall. That side of the bed should be empty.

Oh my god, please let it be empty. Please don't let me not remember actually getting laid. It's been so long I swear my hymen has probably grown back. It's really hard to get any action when Matteo is always hovering around.

Keeping my body as still as I possibly can, I peek one eye open and sigh in relief. Although that relief is short-lived. The body that I'm waking up next to isn't a stranger. No, it's much worse. It's Matteo.

My hands reach under the blanket. I have clothes on. *Thank God.*

"When you're finished having your internal panic attack, let me know and I'll order breakfast." Matteo's husky voice has my head turning back to him. His dark eyes shine with laughter he is clearly trying to hold in.

"I'm not panicking. Why would I need to panic? We didn't do anything... right?" I can't believe I have to ask.

"Yeah, I'm not even going to fucking answer that, Savvy," he snaps and pulls himself out of bed. The door to the bathroom slams shut behind him.

"Think you can slam doors a little quieter?" I yell back, my head now pounding at a punishing level. A minute later, I hear the shower running. Guilt seeps through me. I pissed him off. I know that. I know why too.

I drag my sore and tired self out of bed and open the bathroom door. He doesn't say anything, keeping his back to me as the water cascades down his body. His very naked body. For a moment, I'm stunned speechless. What was I thinking? Of course he's naked in the shower. Still, I couldn't help but walk in. I swear each part of me is at war with itself when it comes to Matteo. My body and soul taking up one side, my mind the other. What frightens me is I don't know which portion is going to win this fight.

"Are you just going to stand there and watch? Or do you wanna climb in?" Matteo looks over his shoulder, catching me staring at his ass through the very clear glass.

"Are you having a cold shower?" I ask him. There's no steam in the room.

"Unfortunately. What do you want, Savvy?"

"I'm sorry. I didn't mean to imply that you would... that we would... I'm sorry." I stumble over my attempt at an apology.

"The fact that you'd even ask, Savvy, pisses me the fuck off. You really think I'd take advantage of you when you're so fucking intoxicated I had to carry your ass back here?"

"No, I don't. It's not you I was worried about. You know there are two of us. What if I took advantage of you?" At this, he turns around fully, and it's taking every ounce of willpower not to look down. To keep my eyes on his face.

"As much as it would have pained me, I would have stopped you." His top lip tips up at the corner. "You can take a peek, Savvy. It's hard because of you."

"What? Oh my god! Too far, Matteo." I pivot and face the opposite direction.

However, before I reach the door, he says, "Just so

we're clear, you can take advantage of me anytime you want, babe. When you're sober. And I wouldn't do a thing to stop you."

"Yeah, that's what I'm afraid of," I mumble, exiting the bathroom. I walk into the living room almost missing the two large bodies, which were certainly not there yesterday, now occupying the sofa. Rocco and Joey, Matteo's shadows. It would bother me more if it didn't mean he was safer having them around.

"Ma'am," Joey says as he stands.

"Don't get up on my account, and it's Savvy. Not *ma'am* but you already know that, Joey." I smile at him, pick up the phone, and order breakfast *for four* to be sent up to the room. "So what are you two doing here? I hardly think anything's going to happen at a wedding full of normals." I refer to those of us who are not part of the underground mafia as the *normal* humans of the world. They hate it, and so does Matteo.

"Ah, can't we just come to see you?" Rocco asks with a grin.

I tilt my head at him. He's good looking, six-foot-something, full of muscles with loads of tatts. I would jump his bones in a heartbeat. I grin at the thought. "I'm not sure you could handle me, Rocco."

His face goes ghost white as a growl echoes through the room. Matteo walks in, fully dressed in a suit. How the hell does he get ready so quickly? And what is he ready for? We don't have to be at the wedding until later this afternoon.

"I know he couldn't handle you, babe, because he'd be fucking dead before he got the chance to even try." Matteo smirks, but the warning is heard loud and clear.

"Sorry, boss." Rocco looks in any other direction than where I'm standing.

"Where are you going?" I ask Matteo, ignoring his threats to his friends.

"I have work to do. I'll be back as soon as I can."

"Matteo, we have plans. Don't make me go to this wedding alone."

"I won't. I promise. Relax. Spend the day in the spa. I'll be back well before we have to leave."

"I just ordered breakfast."

"Uh, I gotta go, Savvy." He nods to Rocco and Joey, and they walk to the elevator. Matteo wraps his arms around me. "Go back to sleep for a bit. It's gonna be a long night." With a light kiss to the top of my head, he pulls away.

I watch as he enters the elevator, then I turn and go back to bed. Sometimes, Matteo does have good ideas.

8

MATTEO

Ponder and deliberate before you make a move.

— Sun Tzu, The Art of War

his place gives me the creeps. I hate jails. You'd think I'd have made my peace with them, considering I could at any point end up in one. But walking through here has my skin crawling. The place reeks of sweat, piss, and desperation and I'm only in the visitation room.

Rocco sits next to me, posing as my legal aide. Tony Gambino was refused bail, deemed a flight risk. Which he is. It'd be way too easy for him to get on one of his many private jets and disappear. If I were in his shoes, I'd be doing just that. Because he's looking at spending the rest of his life in this shithole.

This is not what I was planning for this weekend. I should be spending the day with Savvy; instead, I'm in the last place on earth any made man wants to be. The metal door opens and a worn-out, obviously exhausted Tony Gambino is escorted in, his hands and feet cuffed.

"Is that really necessary? Remove the cuffs," I tell the guards. "Now," I add when none of them move quick enough.

The younger one unlocks the shackles that are wrapped around Tony's ankles, then looks to the other guards for... support? I don't know what he's looking for exactly.

"The hands too, before I file a suit for harassment and unfair treatment of an inmate," I warn them. It's bullshit but most of them aren't educated enough to know that. Besides, it's not the truth that matters, just the conviction of my voice that leaves them with a sense of uncertainty.

Tony smirks at the young guard as the kid unlocks the cuffs around his wrists. The chains fall to the ground in front of us. Stepping over the pile of metal, Tony throws himself down into the seat on the other side of the table.

I look to the guards. "That's all. And I expect those cameras to be turned off immediately," I tell them. I wait for the blinking red light to disappear before I speak again. "RICO, huh?"

"It seems that way."

"What is it that you want me to do here, Gambino? You have a team of defense attorneys."

"They're not one of us. You, you're one of us. I want you to look over the files. Uncover a fucking loophole or something those other useless assholes haven't been able to find," he says.

"A loophole, that's your defense? A loophole?" I laugh. He really is screwed.

"They've been on me for five years. And, now, suddenly they have two eyewitnesses prepared to testify, neither of whom we've been able to track down. They're fucking ghosts. So, yes, a goddamn loophole is what I want. Unless you can find those rat bastards who think they can put me away."

"Well, it kind of seems like they *have* put you away. But don't worry, I'll find your loophole. Have your team send me everything they got. I'll go through it." Pushing to my feet, I do up the button on my jacket.

"Thanks, I appreciate this," he says, shaking my hand.

As soon as I shut the car door, Rocco looks at me. "You really think you can find a loophole?" he asks.

"No, but I sure as shit can mess with the Feds evidence and create one." I smirk. It wouldn't be the first time I've had someone hack into their database and either destroy, plant, or alter evidence to suit my needs. That's not something I was going to share with Tony Gambino though. He doesn't need to know how I'm planning on getting him out of there. Just that I will.

"Where to, boss?"

"The jet. We gotta make a quick trip to Beverly Hills."

"I'll let the pilots know," Joey says, already tapping away at his phone. I lean my head against the seat. This is going to be a fucking long-ass day.

§

"CAN YOU DO IT?" I ask Jasper, the hacker I met in college who never asks questions when I need him to do something.

"Can I do it? Don't insult me, Matteo," he scoffs, already typing away at his keyboard. He has four huge screens spread out in front of him, each displaying code. I don't know what any of that shit means. "You know you could have called. You didn't have to fly all the way here for this."

"Yes, I did," I tell him. I wasn't going to chance phone lines with this request. "How long will it take?"

"Give me a couple of days," he responds.

"Fine. When it's done, come see me in New York." I'm heading back there tomorrow night.

"Deal."

9

SAVVY

Love is patient and kind; love does not envy or boast; it is not arrogant or rude. It does not insist on its own way; it is not irritable or resentful; it does not rejoice at wrongdoing, but rejoices with the truth.

1 Corinthians 13:4–6 (ESV)

He's late. Again.

I'm not surprised. Disappointed, yes. Surprised, not in the slightest. Matteo Valentino is always freaking late. I pick up my phone and check for any missed calls, even a text message, and I've got nothing. I'd call him, but I don't want to be that person. You know, the one who annoys the crap out of people when they're working.

My mind goes to all the worst possible scenarios as to why he could be late. It's never good, and no matter how often I'm left waiting for him, I always fear the worst. The thought that I'm never going to see him again is always in my mind during times like this. I'm almost ready to call in the search party. Maybe reach out to one of his brothers, or his dad. They'd know where he is for sure.

My whole body spins around when I hear the elevator door ping and Matteo swaggers inside the room. Yes, *freaking swaggers*. Like he doesn't have a care in the world.

"I know you own a watch, Matteo, because I gave you one for your birthday," I tell him.

He looks up from his phone, to my face. "I'm sorry. I got here as soon as I could." His eyes roam the length of me. I'm wearing an emerald-green, floor-length, satin dress. It's backless, with thin spaghetti straps that cross over each other at my shoulders. But he hasn't seen that part yet. "Una fottuta bellezza senza sforzo," he says.

Effortlessly fucking beautiful. I do my best not to show him how much his words light embers inside me —embers that need to remain dormant. "Your flattery isn't going to work tonight."

"Savvy, it's not flattery when it's the truth. Come on, let's go."

As much as I'd love to stand here and argue with him, berate him about his lack of time management skills, we're already late. "At this point, we'll be lucky if we get to hear them say I do," I mumble.

⁂

WE ARRIVE at the church just in time. Sneaking in through a side door, we head to the back row of pews as the organ starts playing. "She's beautiful," I whisper to Matteo.

Julie is the picturesque bride. A huge smile lights up her face as she walks down the aisle with her dad. I'll never have that. My father and I don't exactly see eye to eye on anything. Most particularly my friendship with Matteo. I haven't heard from him in over six months.

"Not even close to as beautiful as you are, Savvy," Matteo whispers back. I swear he did an elective course on sweet-talking in college, because he always manages to weasel his way into my good graces.

The bride makes it down the aisle, and everyone takes a seat. I tune out most of what the priest says. That's until he gets to a very familiar bible verse: "Love is patient and kind; love does not envy or boast; it is not arrogant or rude. It does not insist on its own way; it is not irritable or resentful; it does not rejoice at wrongdoing, but rejoices with the truth." Then he closes the book and continues with the ceremony.

I call bullshit on that whole speech. Whoever came up with that obviously did not love Matteo Valentino. If love were patient and kind, then why did God make me love my best friend? What's *kind* about that? To me, it seems like a cruel trick.

If love does not envy or boast, then why is it that I envy what Hunter and Julie have? That normal, safe, boring life. I bet Julie doesn't have to worry about if Hunter's going to come home or not.

It's not arrogant or rude? I've never met a man more arrogant than the one presently beside me.

It does not insist on its own way? That's more on me than Matteo. I do insist on choosing how my life turns out. I will not settle for a future where I'm bound to end up a young widow.

It's not irritable or resentful? Again, that part's on me. If I'm honest with myself, I do resent Matteo for choosing his family over me. Although I would never want him to not do just that. It's that between-a-rock-and-a hard-place type of situation. Damned if you do. Damned if you don't.

"You may kiss the bride." The priest's words bring me out of my own head.

I look over to see Matteo swiping his fingers under his eyes. "Are you crying?" I ask him.

"Don't be ridiculous. I don't fucking cry, Savvy. I have allergies," he grunts.

"Or you're slowly burning from being inside a place of God? You know, since you're one of the devil's minions."

"Funny, you should go into stand-up," he deadpans.

"I thought so." I shrug.

10

MATTEO

Appear weak when you are strong, and strong when you are weak.

– Sun Tzu, The Art of War

S avvy reaches down and clasps her hand around mine, giving it a reassuring squeeze. I'm not sure why. It's fucking allergies. I'm not crying over a fucking wedding. Especially when it's unlikely I'll ever have one of my own.

Shaking off the depressing thoughts, I push to my feet, tugging Savvy up with me. "Thank fuck that shit's over. Now the fun part begins."

"The fun part?" She raises a brow.

I look down to our joined hands. She hasn't pulled away yet. She's always the first to pull away. I'll never let go of her willingly. If she doesn't let go, we'll be joined for life. She must notice where my mind is because, just as that thought flits between my ears, she yanks her hand free.

"The drinking part! That's why people come to weddings, Savvy, the free booze." I smile, even though it's the last thing I feel like doing.

"Right, because you can't afford booze otherwise."

We walk out of the church. I lead her over to the car Rocco and Joey are positioned outside of. As we approach, Rocco opens the back door. I wait for Savvy to climb in before I jump in next to her. I had Joey prepare an ice bucket with a bottle of champagne. I hate the shit, but I know Savvy loves it.

"Are we celebrating?" she asks.

"Yep." I pick up the bottle, unwrapping the foil from the top.

"What are we celebrating?"

Popping the cork, I hold the bottle out so I don't get the shit all over me. I fill a flute to the midway point and hand it to her before pouring myself one too. Then I raise my glass to her and toast, "To undying love."

Her eyes gloss over. "To undying love," she whispers back, quickly bringing the brim to her lips.

"So, ya think we'll have a church wedding when we finally get our shit together?" I ask her.

"What happened to Elvis? He was growing on me."
She laughs.

This is what we do. We joke about us ending up together; we avoid the feelings we actually have for each other because it's easier. I'm not prepared to lose her, and she's not ready for anything other than friendship. At this point, I don't think she ever will be. Still, there's that little flicker of fucking hope that won't let me give up on her.

"We are in Vegas, Savvy. Say the word and I'll have a ring on your finger quicker than you can blink, babe." I tap my glass against hers, then swallow the remaining liquid.

"How about we just go and celebrate our friends, and we can worry about our lives another night," she says, looking out the window while avoiding my gaze.

"Sure, sounds like a fucking blast," I mutter.

"YOU'RE WASTED, like really, really wasted," Savvy yells into my ear. Why she's yelling, I have no idea. The party's finishing up. The happy couple has left for their honeymoon.

"So are you." I pop her on her nose.

"Let's do it," she says.

"Do what?"

"The Elvis thing, let's do it. Right now."

"Are you asking me to marry you, Savannah?

Because if you are, the answer is yes. It will always be a big fat yes!"

"Then, yes—wait." She presses a hand to my chest. "We need a license or something, don't we?"

I pull out the piece of paper that's been burning a hole in my pocket since we arrived. Call me wishful. Fucking pathetic. Whatever. I don't give a shit. I've been carrying around a marriage license for Savvy and me all fucking weekend.

Did I forge her signature to get it? Fuck yes, I did.

Do I regret doing that? Not a fucking chance.

"I have one." I hold the document higher when she goes to reach for it. "Uh, I think I'll keep this." I laugh before tucking it back into my pocket.

"So, are we doing this? Are you actually going to marry me, Matteo Valentino?"

"You know I'd marry you in a heartbeat, Savvy, but why now? I hope you're aware that, if we do this, there's no going back." I pull her into my body.

"I don't want to go back. I want to marry you because you are my soul mate, Matteo. I don't want to waste time. I don't want to look back years from now and wonder *what if*, you know?"

I look into her eyes. We're both wasted. "This is a bad idea. We're drunk. Maybe we should wait until tomorrow," I suggest.

"Are you scared, Tao? Because I don't think I can marry a scaredy-cat anyway."

I laugh, a full belly laugh. The kind only she can manage to get out of me.

HALF AN HOUR LATER, we find ourselves standing in front of an Elvis impersonator. "Place the ring on her finger and repeat after me."

I slide the cheap wedding band onto her finger. "I promise I'll buy you a new one," I tell her.

"I don't need a fancy ring. I love this one. I'm never taking it off." She smiles and stumbles on her feet slightly.

"Okay. I, *state your name…*" Elvis instructs.

"I, Matteo John Valentino…"

"Take, *state her name….*"

"Take Savannah Marie St. James…"

"As my lawfully wedded wife."

I repeat Elvis's words.

"By the power vested in me by the state of Nevada, I now pronounce you man and wife. You may kiss your bride."

I don't have to be told twice. I've been waiting for this moment for fucking years. My lips slam onto hers. Savvy's mouth opens for me. I pick her up bridal-style and carry her out of the chapel.

By the time we exit the elevator, her dress is hitting the floor. I take her hand and we both stumble into the bedroom. She starts to unbutton my shirt. I decide it's taking too long and rip it open, pulling the fabric down my arms and throwing it across the room. Next I undo my belt and the top button of my pants. Then I take a step back and look at her. My bride.

"Una fottuta bellezza senza sforzo," I say. "I fucking love you, Savannah Valentino."

She laughs. "Probably not as much as I love you," she says, climbing onto the bed.

I follow her, straddling her hips. My hands roam up and down her body. A body that is finally mine, a body that I plan to worship all fucking night. Cupping her naked breasts in my hands, I lean down, placing a gentle kiss to the top of each one. "These are mine now, Savvy."

"Ah, pretty sure they're still mine."

I shake my head. "Nope, mine. And this…" I kiss my way down her stomach, keeping my eyes locked on hers. "Mine."

"Yeah? What else is yours?"

I smirk. Sitting upright again, I slide her panties down her thighs. She helps kick them off before opening her legs wide, placing one on each side of my own. My mouth waters as I stare down at her pussy. "This." I run a single finger up her wet slit. "Has always been fucking mine."

"Mmm, maybe you should do something with it

then." She smiles as she reaches for the zipper on my pants. Sliding it lower, she digs her hand inside and wraps it around my cock.

"Fuck, hold that thought." I push to my feet and drop my pants to the floor, kicking my shoes and socks off along the way. My palm fists my cock as I kneel back on the bed before positioning myself between her thighs. "Are you sure you want this, Savvy?" I ask her, pumping myself a few times.

"Are you sure you want this?" she asks, running her own hands up and down her body.

"There's never been a doubt in my mind, babe." I want to fucking lick, bite, and suck every inch of her skin. But, more than that, I want to bury my dick inside that sweet fucking pussy of hers. I push in slowly. My eyes roll to the back of my head. Leaning down, I capture her lips with mine. "Fuck, Savvy, you're so fucking perfect." I slam home. She's so fucking wet and ready for me.

"Fuck me, Matteo," she says, wrapping her legs around my waist.

"I don't want to fuck you. I want to make love to you," I tell her. "I want this to last forever."

"And you can, next time. Right now, I need you to make me come. Please." Her hands circle around my neck, pulling my mouth back onto hers.

"With fucking pleasure," I grit out between kisses. Pushing up on my knees, I lift her legs and rest her ankles on my shoulders before leaning forward again. I can feel my cock go even deeper inside her. Her back arches off the bed and I swear she looks like a fucking angel. Her blonde hair fans out around her like a halo. Her pale skin glistens with a sheen of light sweat. "Hold on, babe. This ride's going to be a rough one."

"Yes!" she moans as I circle my hips, grinding my pelvis down onto her clit. Pulling free, I thrust back in fast, hard, then circle my hips again when I bottom out. "Oh god, Matteo. Don't stop," she screams.

"Don't plan to," I grunt, repeating the motion over and over while quickening my pace until I feel her whole body tighten up. Her pussy squeezes the fuck out of my cock.

I can't hold back anymore. I explode, falling off that cliff face-first with her.

11

SAVVY

Therefore what God has joined together, let no one separate.

Mark 10:9

*S*hit, shit, double shit! *What on earth did I do?* I peek an eye open. Matteo lies flat on his back, his tanned toned pecs stretched out with one arm covering his eyes. My heart hurts for what I'm about to do.

I slide out of the bed. I don't want to. I don't want to run, but I can't seem to stop myself. I hate myself for fleeing. Again. But I also don't know any other way to protect my heart. To protect myself from the hurt that'll happen if I stay.

It might not happen today, but it *will* happen. I'll get comfortable. I'll get complacent and then I'll lose him. I'll lose everything. So I do the only thing I can. I throw on a pair of sweats and a shirt. I pick up my shoes and tiptoe out of the door. I count down the seconds as I wait for the elevator to reach this floor, sighing in relief when the doors finally close and the carriage begins its descent. My heart pounds, and my stomach twists. I should go back up there. I should just talk to him. He'll understand. I know he will.

I keep telling myself to go back, but when the doors open into the lobby, I run. Hailing the first cab I see, I jump in the back seat. "Where to?" the driver asks.

Good question. Where exactly am I going?

"Ah, the airport," I tell him. Opening the search browser on my phone, I pull up the first flight from Las Vegas to New York. There isn't anything for hours. By the time I get on one of those, Matteo will have found me. I need to get out of this city. I have one option. Only one. My father.

I press the green dial button and wait for him to answer. "Savannah? What can I do for you?" he greets me with a questioning tone.

No hello. No how've you been... Just straight down to business. What do you want?

"I need the jet. Can you have it ready to fly me back to New York in twenty minutes?"

There's silence on his end for a moment. I'm about to hang up. It was a mistake to think that he'd help me. "Are you in trouble?" he asks.

"No, I just forgot I had a very important meeting, and I can't get a flight out of Vegas that will make it back in time." The lie slips from my lips easily.

"I didn't realize you were in town. We should have met for dinner," he says.

"I'm only here for a quick trip, a friend's wedding," I respond, while my mind replays the *other* wedding that transpired last night.

"Okay. Meet Jordan at the hanger. He'll fly you home," Dad says.

"Thank you."

"And, Savannah?"

"Yes?"

"If you're in trouble, I do hope you know you can come to me for help whenever you need it." His words choke me up. My father has never told me this before. I think, somewhere in the back of my mind, I knew. I knew I could go to him. Though I don't think I've ever really doubted that he would help me. He'd just gloat and give me a million *I told you sos* in the process.

"Thank you, Dad. I do know that." I hang up.

"Change of plans. Can you take me to the North Las Vegas airport instead please?" I ask the cabbie.

"Sure thing, ma'am," he says.

"Thank you." I lean my head back and close my eyes.

What the hell am I doing? My leg shakes with nerves. *Please don't hate me, Matteo.*

I stare at my phone in my hand. I should turn it off. I know the minute he wakes up, he's going to call, message me. Demand to know where I am. I have no idea what I'm going to say to him once he does manage to catch up with me. I can just imagine it now: *Hey, so how about a divorce? An annulment?*

Somehow I don't think he's going to be as receptive to those requests as I'd like him to be. I don't want to hurt him. I love him. I really do. I just know I won't survive him. I'm not cut out to be the kind of wife he needs, the kind of wife who can handle the world he lives in. I struggle coping most days just being his best friend. The constant worry—the knowledge that he's out in the city doing things that could possibly get him killed or sent to prison—is not easy to live with.

I honestly don't know how his mother does it. Holly Valentino is the sweetest woman I've ever met. I remember how much she helped me when I was twelve and my own mother died. Holly was there for me whenever I needed her. I've always been able to talk to her. She taught me about periods, when I was thirteen and phoned Matteo crying. He didn't know what to do so he sent his mom over to my house. Holly even took me dress shopping for prom. And she was the one who screamed and cheered for me at my graduations.

Sure, my dad was in the crowd too, but you wouldn't have known it. It was the Valentino family who acted like I'd just cured cancer each time I walked across the stage. I want nothing more than to call her now, ask her for advice. Let her tell me what I should do. Except this time is different. I just ran off and eloped with her son. How the hell am I supposed to go to her with that?

There isn't anyone I can go to. There isn't anyone who will understand how I feel. I just need to figure this out. On my own. Somehow.

§.

I EXPECTED my phone to be buzzing with incoming messages and calls from Matteo when I landed in New York, but it's been radio silent. It's odd, and I'm both grateful and worried. What if something happened to him after I left? What if he's finally had enough and is going to cut all ties with me?

I really didn't think this through very well. I can't lose his friendship. I can't lose him. However, I also know I can't be married to him.

I jump in the car that's waiting for me when I land, thinking my father must have ordered it. It's not until the door closes that I realize my mistake. "Ma'am, how was your flight?" A familiar face greets me through the rearview mirror.

"Wh-What are you doing here, Rocco?" I try the door handle but it doesn't budge. "Unlock the door, Rocco."

85

"Sorry, boss's orders, ma'am," he says as the car starts moving.

"What orders?" I ask. Rocco looks at me and smiles. He won't answer. I knew he wouldn't. There's nothing I can do but sit back and wait to be delivered to *the boss*. "Is he okay?" I continue after a few minutes of silence.

"Define *okay*?" Rocco replies.

I don't respond. By that answer, I know Matteo is losing his mind.

Fifteen minutes later, the car stops out front of my apartment building. I'm confused but I'm not about to question it. Maybe I can at least shower, change my clothes, and come up with what the hell I'm going to say to Matteo. Sagging against the elevator wall, I count each of the floors until the doors finally open on mine.

I half expected Rocco to follow me inside, but when I looked back, he was still stationed at the building's entrance. Unlocking the door, I walk into my apartment and stop in my tracks as my eyes land on a very pissed off Matteo currently standing in my foyer.

MATTEO

In the midst of chaos, there is also opportunity.

– Sun Tzu, The Art of War

I've felt this kind of betrayal before. The first time I woke up after we finally gave in to each other, and Savvy was gone. I'm a fucking idiot for thinking this time would be any different. It is fucking different though. I didn't just spend a night of passion with my best friend. I spent the night with my fucking wife. She doesn't get to run again. I won't let her.

I knew when I woke up and she wasn't in the bed that she'd fled again. And I knew she'd come back to her apartment. I didn't have to track her phone to know that. I also knew I'd beat her there. Here. judging by the shock on her face right now, she underestimated me. She thought she'd have time before I chased her down.

"Good flight?" I ask her. My hands fist in my pockets. I want to reach out and grab her. Pull her up against me. But I don't. Not yet.

"What's going on?" she questions, peeking behind me.

I have ten guys sorting through her things. There are boxes everywhere. "I'm helping you pack." I smile.

"Stop. Tell them to leave, Matteo. Now." She throws her bag down on the entry table.

"No."

Her eyes widen. I think we're both shocked that I just uttered those words. "What do you mean no?" She positions her hands on her hips.

"I mean *no*. I'm not telling them to stop. Your shit needs packing. What kind of *husband* would I be if I left it all for you to do?" I raise an eyebrow at her. I also don't fucking miss the way she flinches when I uttered that word. *Husband.*

"We need to talk about this, Matteo. Alone. Tell them to leave," she says.

"Oh, we're going to talk all right. Just as soon as we get home."

"I am home," she hisses.

Tilting my head to the side, I eye her up and down. "No, you're not. Put your shoes back on. We're leaving."

"You can leave, along with all these assholes touching my things. I'm staying. Don't let the door slam you on the way out, Matteo." She tries to step around me.

My arm snakes out lightning fast and encircles her waist. Pulling her up close, I lean down to her ear. "It wasn't a fucking request, Savannah. Put your shoes on and walk out that door with me or I'll fucking carry you out."

She squirms against my hold. "Let me go."

"Yeah, that's never going to fucking happen," I grunt. I do release her though, spin her around, and point down at her shoes on the floor. "So what's it going to be?"

Savvy pivots to glare at me. Whatever she sees in my eyes has her submitting. For now at least. She slides her feet into her shoes. And without saying another word, she storms out her front door and stomps towards the elevator. I follow closely behind her. If she thinks she's going to get the opportunity to run again, she's sorely mistaken. We descend in silence. I can't help but smile at how she attempts to keep as much space between us as she can. I let her have it. She's about to find out just how little distance between us there will be from now on. As soon as I get her alone.

When the elevator doors open, I step forward and take hold of her hand. She jerks her arm away, trying to free herself. I smile at her and tighten my grip. "Can't have you trying to be a runaway bride, now, can I?" I pull her towards the exit as she curses me out under her breath. I open the back door of the waiting SUV. "Get in." Savvy scans her surroundings. "No one here is going to stop me from picking you up and throwing you inside, Savvy, which I will if I have to," I warn her.

I see the anger in her eyes. She's fuming but she also knows I'm telling the truth. With a glare that would weaken most men, she climbs into the back seat. When I hop in after her, she slides right across to the other side, practically hugging the door. I can't help but laugh. Which only infuriates her further.

"I swear to God, Matteo, you are going to regret this," she growls out.

"My only regret, Savvy, is not marrying your ass sooner," I tell her.

"You can't be serious. We can't do this, Tao. We can't."

"Too late. We already did."

She turns to stare out the window as Rocco pulls away from her apartment building, or should I say her *former* apartment building. She won't be coming back.

Two hours later, we pull up to a gated estate. Rocco enters the code into the panel and drives up the long, winding path. "Where are we?" Savvy asks.

"Home." I smile.

"This isn't your apartment, Matteo. Where are we?"

"I told you. Home. I bought this place a few years ago."

"I've never seen it. Why haven't I been here before?" she asks, staring at the looming mansion.

"I was waiting for the right time to show you." I shrug. When the car stops, I open the door, lean back in, and hold out my hand. She looks at it like it's going to bite her if she takes it. "Savvy, really? You think it's going to hurt you?" I feign sarcasm but secretly I'm annoyed she actually looks scared.

"Of course not. I just don't want to hold your hand right now." She slides out of the car. Her open palms land on my chest as she pushes me back a step. Without warning, I bend forward and pick her up, throwing her over my shoulder. "Put me down! What the hell are you doing?" Her fists pound on my back.

"Carrying my bride over the fucking threshold. Stop hitting me, Savvy." I slap her ass.

"Ow, fuck, Matteo, stop. Put me down. You're being freaking ridiculous," she yells.

Opening the door, I walk inside, slamming it shut with my foot. "I'll give you the tour later," I tell her as I climb the staircase.

"I don't want the tour. I want to go home," she says right before her teeth latch on to my hip.

"Did you just fucking bite me?" I grunt.

"Yes, and I'll do it again if you don't freaking put me

91

down now!" she screams. Her words echo off the walls.

I've only had one room furnished in this house. I always knew that this would be my and Savvy's home, and I wasn't about to have another interior designer furnish it for her. The bedroom, however, I had done. I've slept here a few times when I've needed to get away from everyone, and I refused to sleep on the fucking floor.

When I step inside, I throw Savvy down on the bed. She scoots up immediately, crawling to the opposite side of the mattress. As far away from me as she can get. Once again. "What on earth are you thinking?" she says, climbing down and straightening out her shirt.

"I was thinking that I'm bringing my wife home to show her the house I bought for us. You know most women would be overjoyed to get a place like this as a wedding gift."

"Okay, stop. Matteo, this is a joke. You and I both know we can't stay married. Last night was..." Her words trail off.

"Your decision," I say, reminding her that it was, in fact, her idea to get hitched by Elvis.

"I know, but I was drunk. And so were you... We just need to get an annulment or something, and then things can go back to how they were."

"No," I tell her.

"What? You can't say no. You're a lawyer, Matteo. You can file the paperwork yourself. We don't even need to tell anyone. To get anyone else involved."

SAVVY

Love must be sincere. Hate what is evil;
cling to what is good.

Romans 12:9

"*I* will never give you a divorce, Savvy. You're wasting your breath even asking for one." Matteo slips his hands into his pockets. His head tips downwards and he gazes at the floor. I know that pose. He's hurt. I get it. It's not like I'm not hurting myself here too.

"Matteo, what happens next week when you decide you're done with me? When you decide that you're ready for a new, more exciting adventure?" I ask him.

I've never known Matteo to be in a relationship with anyone. I know he sleeps around. It's not like it's hard for him. One look at the man, and women throw their panties in his direction. Literally. I've seen it more than once.

"That's not going to happen. You and I both know that's not what you're worried about." He runs a hand through his hair, ruffling his dark locks. "Spit it out. Tell me what you're afraid of, Savvy, because I'm really starting to lose my fucking patience here."

"We just work better as friends. You know that."

"How are you so sure? We've never tried to be anything more," he counters.

"I just know. I'm not the wife you need, Matteo."

"You're right. You're not the wife I need. You're the fucking wife I want. You're the wife I've got." He starts walking towards the threshold.

"Where are you going?"

"Downstairs, before I say something I can't take back." He slams the door without glancing my way again.

And I'm left standing here. In the middle of a room. That has Matteo written all over it. Right down to the oversized king bed, with navy-blue and white bedding. A large dark-mahogany chest of drawers sits along one wall. There're two doors opposite the dresser and one across from me—I head towards the singular door, swing it open, and my mouth drops.

It's a bathroom, but it's not just any bathroom. It's my bathroom.

Well, not mine, but it's the bathroom I have pinned up on the vision board of my dream home. It's exactly what I wanted, right down to the white and grey marble double sink with black faucets. There's a large oval tub, surrounded by floor-to-ceiling windows that overlook a luscious green garden. Walking farther into the room, I see that the shower's hidden behind a spacious white-tiled wall. That's not what captures my attention though. It's the large letters in sparkling black stone. Right in the center, spelling out our initials: MSV.

That wasn't on the vision board. That's all Matteo's doing. He really did all this? He had my dream bathroom constructed right here?

I don't know what to think. My heart is aching. I want to go find him, wrap my arms around him, and never let go. But I know that's a dream, no matter what he says. I know he'll always belong to the family first and me second.

Why is this so freaking hard?

I walk out of the bathroom, refusing to let the tears fall. I need to shut down this emotional crap. I need to stand strong. It's the only way I know how to survive. Opening the first door on the far side of the room, I enter the empty wardrobe—a very impressive, empty wardrobe. This space alone is larger than the living room in my apartment. Closing the door, I open the other one. It mirrors the empty closet space, only this one has clothes and accessories in it. Matteo's clothes and accessories.

My fingers roam over the fabric of the shirts lining the hangers, in freaking color-coded order. I take a white shirt, bring it to my face, and inhale. It smells like his laundry detergent. I need to get a grip. I need to get out of this place and go home. I quickly shut the closet door and walk over to the one Matteo slammed behind him. I open it and find myself standing on a large landing area. There's a double staircase to my right and a long hallway with numerous closed doors to my left.

I don't need to know what's behind those doors. What I need is to get out of here. I walk down the stairs. Standing in the foyer, I spin around to get the full view. It's pretty. Expansive. And striking. If I were to pluck my dream home out of a magazine, this would be it. A huge silver chandelier hangs from the center of the ornate ceiling. It's mesmerizing, my eyes inspecting how all of the swirls intertwine with each other.

"You like it?" Matteo's voice makes me jump ten feet in the air.

"It's beautiful," I whisper, still in awe as I take in my opulent surroundings.

"Good. Anything you don't like can be changed. Just say the word." He says it like it's a done deal, me living here.

"I'm not staying, Matteo. I can't."

He tilts his head to the side, much like he'd done

earlier. "Do you really think I'm just going to let you walk out of here? You're my wife, Savvy, whether you like that or not. It's a fact. It's legal. I made sure of that." He pauses, taking a step closer to me.

"Well, *un*legalize it, Matteo. I know you can do that."

"I could, but I won't. Unless you can give me one damn good reason why I should," he says.

I take a breath and release it. "I don't love you. You shouldn't be stuck with a wife who doesn't love you." The lie tastes bitter on my tongue.

"That." Matteo points at me. "Would be a great reason. If it were true."

I stand frozen to my spot as he takes another step forward. His hand comes up and cups my cheek. His thumb brushes against my lower lip. My breath hitches, my pulse goes into overdrive, and I can feel the flush working its way up my neck.

"Even when you lie to me, you're fucking breathtakingly beautiful, Savvy," he says, right before his lips slam over my mouth.

I gasp and then feel his tongue begin to war with mine. It's like my body takes over and my brain gets left behind. My arms have a mind of their own as they circle his neck and tug him closer to me.

Matteo nibbles on my lower lip before he pulls away. "You can lie to me all you want, but I know you, Savvy. Better than you know yourself." He shrugs.

What can I say to that? He does know me, but he

can't know what I'm really afraid of. There's no way. I've never voiced it.

"So, Mrs. Valentino, what do you want for dinner? I'm cooking." Matteo smiles at me.

I feel my face pale. My body starts to shake. Am I in shock? About to have some kind of seizure? I have no idea, but all of a sudden, I can't breathe.

"Fuck! Savannah, fucking breathe, damn it."

I look around. I can hear Matteo, but he sounds like he's underwater. I feel myself being lifted and then I'm moving, but I don't know where I'm going. I close my eyes. "I can't... Mat... teo... I..." I can't even get the words out.

"It's okay. I've got you, Savvy. You're okay. Just breathe."

I can feel his hands running up and down my back. After a while, I open my eyes and see Matteo looking back at me.

"You're okay. You know I'd never let anything hurt you, Savvy, right?"

"I know that you believe that," I tell him.

"So, was it the prospect of my cooking that made you literally have a panic attack or just the whole Mrs. Valentino thing?"

"I can't do this, Matteo. Please, don't make me do this," I beg him.

"Ask me for anything and I'll find a way to give it to you. But I'm not giving you a divorce. I'm not giving up on us. We're meant to be, always have been."

I shake my head. I can't form the words I need to say. I know it's useless. I can see he has made up his mind, and once Matteo has set his sights on something, he doesn't give up.

Basically, I have two choices: Go along with this insanity of his, trusting that we'll actually end up a happily married couple and wait for my heart to be broken and torn to shreds. OR... break his heart and walk away from him for good.

Neither are options I want. What I want is to wake up and for this all to be a dream. For us to be the same as we were yesterday. Just Matteo and Savvy, the best of friends.

As if he can read my mind, he says, "You're my best friend, Savvy. You're the one good thing I have in my life, and I don't plan on ever letting that go." Matteo wraps his arms around me, and I bury my head in his chest. "Our love is sincere, and it's something we need to cling to, not run from."

Is he right?

He can't be. I've seen what happens when people give into this kind of love. It never ends well.

MATTEO

Who wishes to fight must first count the cost.

— Sun Tzu, The Art of War

*I*t's fucking harder than I thought it would be. Not giving in and letting Savvy walk out. I can't stomach seeing her like this. She hates me right now, or at least is trying to hate me.

She barely touched her dinner. We sat on the kitchen floor because the house has no fucking furniture. I know she's struggling with whatever inner demons she's fighting. I wish she'd just open up and tell me. I don't know how to fucking help her if she doesn't tell me. I'm also petrified that my coming on too strong is going to be the thing that makes me lose her for good. I can't just sit by and wait any longer though. I need to uncover what her fucking hold-up is and figure out a way to get her to move past it. There isn't any other option. I won't lose her.

I walk into the bedroom and find Savvy sitting up with her back pressed to the headboard. Her hair hangs loose over her shoulders, still wet from the shower she just took. "How's the shower?"

"It's fine," she answers. "Where's my bag, Tao? I need my phone," she asks.

I pause. I've purposely kept it from her. She could call anyone and find a way to leave here. Leave me. I'm not stupid. This isn't the first time I've held someone captive, even if that's not what we're calling this. I don't plan on letting her go, though, so it's not much different either. "Ah, I'm not sure," I tell her while approaching the bed.

"You're lying," she says. "Just give me my phone, Matteo."

"Why? So you can call someone to come and save you? I don't think so." I peel back the blanket, revealing her smooth creamy legs. I keep my eyes locked on hers as I separate her thighs, kneeling between them. "No one can save you from this, Savvy. You are mine now and I'm yours."

"But you're not really mine, are you, Matteo? I'll

always come second to your family. You'll never be able to put me first."

Her words have my hands stilling. Is that really what she thinks? "You've been carrying that around a while, huh?" I raise an eyebrow at her. "Savvy, hear me when I say this. I love my family, and yes, I'd do anything for them. Fuck, I'd burn the whole world to the ground and relight it for any one of my brothers. Cousins. My parents." My fingers start their journey up her inner thighs. "But you, you are a part of that family too. You are my family too and it didn't take a piece of paper for that. You've always been my family, Savvy. And you'll always be my fucking number one priority." Her eyes stay on mine. I can tell she's processing my words. She wants to believe them but won't let herself. "Well, that is until we have kids. Then you'll be sharing that spot with our spawn."

"*Our spawn*? Matteo, if you think I'm having kids with you, you're out of your mind. You're forgetting I've known you since you were six. There is no way I'm raising a mini you."

"And you're forgetting you've loved me since you were six. Like it or not, babe, you'll be the mother of our devilish children."

"Matteo, where's my phone? I really do need it— and my laptop. I have work to do."

"You don't have to be at work until tomorrow. Tonight, I want you to shut off all your arguments, all your hold-ups, and just be... us." My hands are almost at the top of her thighs. I can feel the tremor in her legs the closer my fingers get to her pussy.

"We shouldn't do this. It won't change my mind, Matteo."

"Ouch, way to hurt a guy's ego, babe." I smirk.

"I think your ego can handle the blow."

I laugh. Even when we're in the middle of a fight, we always seem to find our way back to each other. To our normal banter. Although this isn't really one of our usual disagreements. This is more of a *changing our lives for the better* kind of moment.

"We should stop." Her words are whispered, and although she's voicing her protests, her legs open wider, inviting me in.

"You don't want me to stop. You know I can make you feel good. You really are wound up, Savvy. Let me help you relax." I lean forward, my lips traveling a path up her left leg, from her knee all the way to the apex of her thighs. Biting and nibbling as I go. My plan was to repeat the process. That is, until I reached the top and discovered she's not wearing any panties. "Fuck. Fottimi, ho appena trovato il paradiso." My tongue slides through her wet folds.

I look up and connect eyes with her, trying to show her everything I'm feeling in this moment. How much I fucking worship her. How much I fucking need her. She breaks the eye contact, falling back against the headboard. She's not telling me to stop anymore though. So I'll take that as a win.

Pulling on her hips, I slide her body down so she's lying flat on the bed. "Better get comfy, babe. I'm going to be here for a while."

"Oh god."

My tongue slides in, and I fucking moan. I will never get enough of her taste. Pushing my tongue as deep as I can go, I flick it around. She's so wet. Her juices cover my chin as I devour her. Replacing my tongue with my fingers, I latch on to her clit with my mouth. Her hips buck up, and her hands cling to my hair. Savvy's thighs squeeze the sides of my head, holding me in place—not that she needs to. I curl my fingers upwards and stroke against that magic spot, and seconds later, her whole body stiffens as she screams out my name. I smile into her pussy. Her screams are music to my ears. I want to hear them over and over again. I continue to lick her as she comes down from her high, and when I feel her whole body relax, I kneel over and claim her mouth. Her hands roam along my naked chest, abs, around my back.

"Fuck!" The feel of her hands on me is too much. I don't want tonight to be about me. I want her to know I'm in this for her, that she's my sole focus. Pulling away, I roll over and lie next to her before wrapping an arm around her waist, making her the little spoon to my big spoon. I reach down and bring the blankets up to cover the both of us.

"Wh-what are you doing?" Savvy attempts to move, to wiggle out of my hold.

Squeezing tighter, I manage to keep her in place. "We're going to sleep, Savvy. Night."

"That's it? We're just going to sleep?" She sounds almost disappointed.

"Yes, we both have work tomorrow. Go to sleep." I kiss the top of her shoulder. We lie in silence for a while, her wiggling hips doing nothing to help my raging boner.

"Matteo?" Savvy whispers.

"Yeah, babe?"

"I'm sorry I ran again." Her words wash over me.

I might not know what's going on in that beautiful fucking head of hers, but there's no doubt that she wants this. She wants us. "I know you are, babe. Go to sleep. We'll talk about this tomorrow."

I wait for her to fall asleep. Once I'm certain she's out of it, I roll over, reach into the bedside drawer, and retrieve the pair of handcuffs I placed in there earlier. Repositioning myself, I hook one side of the cuffs onto Savvy's wrist, the other onto my own. I'm not taking the chance of her running off before I fucking wake up again. I don't care if I have to cuff her to me every night for the rest of our lives. If this is how it has to be, I'm happy to oblige.

SAVVY

Above all, love each other deeply, because love covers over a multitude of sins.

1 Peter 4:8

It's hot. Why am I so hot? It's the middle of winter. I shouldn't be this hot. I roll over or at least I attempt to roll over. There's a heavy weight on me, and something sharp pulls against my wrist when I try to lift my arm. Slowly blinking my eyes open, I see what's digging into my skin. A handcuff. A metal freaking handcuff is closed around my wrist, the other side attached to a much larger and much tanner arm.

"Matteo!" I growl, shoving my elbow into his ribs as hard as I can.

"Ow, fuck! What the hell?" he groans, curling into himself and pulling me along so that I land on top of him.

"What the hell is this?" I hold up my wrist, his arm rising along with mine.

The bastard looks at our joined limbs and smirks. I'm about to tear into him, and he's lying here looking pretty damn proud of himself. "I wasn't taking any chances that you wouldn't be here when I woke up." He shrugs.

"Unlock them now, Matteo," I grit out between clenched teeth. "I can't believe you! This is unnecessary." I shake my arm, which only makes the cuff dig into my wrist harder.

"Okay, but first answer one question." He waits for my nod of agreement before he continues. "Was it that bad?"

"Was what that bad?" I have no idea what he's talking about. I raise an eyebrow, and he clarifies, "Waking up next to me and not running?"

"It's not the waking up next to you part that makes me want to run. It's the *what happens now* part of the equation that engages my fight or flight response," I tell him.

"What is it that you're really afraid of?"

"I don't want to end up like him," I say. I've never told Matteo this—never told anyone.

His gaze sears right through my soul. I see the moment he recognizes my true fear because his whole face shifts. His free hand wraps around my neck, pulling me forward. Closer to him. "You will never end up like him, Savvy. You're not him."

He can't know that. I'm my father's daughter. My body is made up of fifty percent of his DNA. There's a high chance I could end up just like him. "You don't know that," I say it aloud this time. "I was there. I watched what happened to him when my mom died. I watched him break apart. I was there when he became a bitter, angry version of himself."

"You are not going to end up like him. You will never lose me, Savvy."

"Every day you leave, each time you walk out that door, there's a chance you won't come back. My heart can't take it. It's bad now. When we're just friends. But if I let myself be more, if I let myself have you, I know I won't survive it when I lose you."

"Savvy, we're not just friends. That ring on your finger, it's fucking staying there. You are my wife; you are my family. And if something were to happen to me, I promise I'll still be with you. You really think I wouldn't come back and ghost-fuck the shit out of you? I'll follow you everywhere you go. I won't rest in whatever hell I'm destined for until you take your last breath."

"That's... twisted, Tao. You can't control the afterlife."

He reaches over to the bedside table and picks up a key. Then he unlocks the cuffs, takes my hand in his, and rubs the red marks left on my skin. Lifting my wrist to his mouth, he feathers kisses along the indentations.

I know Matteo can be tender, caring, and sweet. Well, towards me anyway. And I usually pull away from him. However, now, I find myself wanting to lean into it. Into him. I find myself wanting to take comfort in this tender side of him. It confuses the hell out of me. So I change the narrative to one I can control.

Pulling free of his hold, I shimmy down until I'm straddling his thighs. My hands travel along his chest, down his abs. Matteo watches my every movement. I have no doubt he's ready to catch me if I jump up and run. I'm not going to, though. At least not yet.

When my fingers reach the waistband of his briefs, I slip them inside. "Savvy, you really shouldn't start anything you don't intend to finish," he warns.

"Don't worry, Tao, I have every intention of *finishing*." I smile as I pull his black briefs down, revealing his cock. His hard, weeping cock. Enclosing my hand around the base, I slide it up and down as I lower my mouth to him. Running my tongue up the underside, I swirl it around when I reach the top before I wrap my lips around him. I do my best to take him all in. I can't, so my hand grips the bottom of his shaft and I pump as I suck him in and out.

"Fuck, Savvy. Fuck me," he curses. Matteo's hands

grip my hair and he holds the loose strands aside as he watches my progress. Our eyes stay connected as I continue to worship him. I feel myself getting wetter the longer I have him in my mouth. The more I see him coming unraveled, the harder I try to make him explode. I want to be the reason he loses control. I want to give him the mind-blowing pleasure he gave me last night. His cock pulls from my mouth with a plop when he releases my hair. He grips my underarms and drags me up his body.

"I wasn't finished with that," I pout.

"I know, but I don't want to come in your mouth, Savvy," he says as he positions my hips over his. Holding his cock to the entrance of my bare pussy, he slowly guides my body down until I'm fully seated on him. My head tips back and a groan parts my lips as I relish the feeling of being fully stretched out. The sting slowly subsides and my hips start to shift on their own. Rocking back and forth. "Fuck, I love how your pussy grips my fucking cock, Savvy."

His fingers lift the hem of my shirt—technically it's one of his shirts—and he raises it over my head, then tosses it aside. He palms my breasts, squeezing the flesh before his fingertips twist and pull at my nipples, sending electric waves straight to my clit.

"Oh god." I grind down on him, trying to get the friction my body is desperately seeking. Matteo releases my breasts and grips my hips. His fingers tighten as he picks me up and slams me back down. "Do that again," I tell him.

He doesn't need to be told twice. He repeats the movement, over and over until I'm coming apart. My pussy quivers, spasming around him. "Fuck me, Savvy. We're waking up like this every goddamn. Fucking. Morning. From. Now. On," he grunts out with each thrust as he comes with me. My body collapses on top of his and I bury my head in the crook of his neck.

I don't have it in me to argue with him right now, so I don't.

16

MATTEO

The supreme art of war is to subdue the enemy without fighting.

— Sun Tzu, The Art of War

"**I**'ll be there as soon as I can, Theo. Not a fucking minute before." I hang up on my brother, spin around, and choke on the coffee that I was just about to swallow. Savvy is standing in the entryway of the kitchen. She's wearing—actually I don't know what the fuck she's wearing or where the hell she got it from. "That's not what I left on the bed for you," I say once I've finished almost succumbing to my self-imposed death.

"Oh, I know. I improvised. You can send those clothes back to the nunnery you stole them from." She walks up and takes the coffee cup from my hands.

I watch, speechless and honestly a little distracted by her ass, as she turns around, opens the fridge, and pours vanilla creamer into what was my coffee. "Ah, babe. You're not leaving this house dressed like that," I tell her, realizing too late that those are probably going to be my last words. But she's out of her pretty little mind if she thinks I'm letting any motherfucker see her like... *this*. She's wearing one of my white dress shirts. I think it was a shirt anyway, seeing as she's tied a knot on one side of it so it sits up high on one of her legs.

Savvy turns around, sipping the coffee with a raised brow. I wait. It's really all I can do. I need to figure out a way to make her more agreeable with me. Maybe I just need to keep her dosed-up on orgasms. It's not like it'd be a hardship. After what feels like hours, she places the cup on the counter and squares her shoulders, preparing herself for a battle she's not about to win. At least I think she's not going to win.

"Matteo, this is never going to happen. When have you ever cared what I wore before anyway?"

"I've always cared. You just weren't my wife before. Now you are."

"Well, I'm going to work dressed like this. You're going to go do whatever it is you do. And while you're at it, you're going to draw up those divorce papers so we can go back to the way things used to be."

"Rocco will take you to work and he'll bring you right back here this afternoon," I tell her. Sometimes you have to pick your battles, win fights without actually *fighting*. This is one of those times. I wrap my hand around her neck and pull her towards me, slamming my lips on hers before she can refute my demands. My tongue dives into her mouth and I kiss her until I feel her knees wobble and her body sink into me. I pull away to smile down at her. "See you tonight, babe. Love you." As I take a step back, I grab the white material that I'm still assuming used to be one of my shirts and rip it in half right down the front.

"Oh my god!" she squeals. I jump back just in time to dodge the palm that comes up to slap me.

"Sorry, babe, gotta go." I slip past her outstretched arms, leaving her to scream after me. Once I make it to the car, I stop in front of Rocco. "Don't leave her side. Make sure she ends up back here tonight in one piece."

"Sure thing, boss," he says, looking at the house where Savvy is still cursing me out at the top of her lungs. "Am *I* going to make it back in one piece?" he questions me.

"Yeah, I can't promise that. Good luck." I jump in my car and drive away with a smile on my face. I always knew being married to Savvy wouldn't be boring.

THE DRIVE back into the city went quicker than I thought it would. The fact that I broke every speed limit to get here helped. When Theo called this morning, he didn't seem like he was in his usual sparkly mood. Come to think of it, my brother doesn't have a sparkly mood. Ever. The asshole is way too fucking serious. He could use some *spark* in his life.

I walk into the office building, where I was instructed to meet him. Theo pretty much oversees all of the Valentino businesses, both legitimate and not even close to being legitimate—probably why he always looks like he has the weight of the world on his shoulders. As much as his grumpy ass grates on my nerves, he's one of the best fucking people I know.

"Good morning, Mr. Valentino." A secretary, whose name I can't remember, stands to greet me as I make my way past her.

"Morning, ma'am." I smile briefly before focusing my gaze on the bank of elevators ahead. I'm a married man now. I can't be giving these women the impression that I'm interested, and judging by the way that secretary was squeezing her breasts together, that's exactly what she was hoping for—my interest. I hit the button for the elevator and pull my phone out of my pocket while I wait. There's a message from Savvy.

MY WIFE:

> Don't forget those papers, Matteo.

Stepping into the elevator, I type out a quick reply.

ME:

> Have a great day at work, babe. See you tonight.

MY WIFE:

> The papers, Matteo. I'm not kidding.

ME:

> Yeah, it didn't feel like you were kidding when you were coming all over my cock this morning either. But don't worry, babe, I plan on a repeat performance tonight.

I see the 'read' indication on the message I sent, then the three little dots appear and disappear a few times before they just stop. I step out of the elevator and walk down the hall. Theo's secretary is on the phone when I walk past her. She smiles and waves me in, not that I was waiting for her permission to enter. I knock out an obnoxious pattern as loud as I can before opening the door.

"Really, Matteo, was that necessary?" Theo grumbles.

"I thought so." I laugh, walk over to the wet bar, and pour myself a glass of whiskey.

"It's nine o'clock in the morning." Theo makes a show of looking at the gold Rolex on his wrist.

"Your point?" I ask and down the contents of my glass in one go.

"Never mind. Come sit. I need you to review these contracts." He slams a manila folder onto the desk in front of him.

"Great, just what I want to be doing on a Monday morning. Going through contracts." I lower myself down on one of the chairs and pick up the folder.

"You're the one who became an attorney, not me."

"I'm a criminal defense attorney, not someone who specializes in corporate law," I point out.

"It's a simple contract, Matteo. I'm sure even your intelligence level can handle it."

I open the folder and read the top of the first piece of paper. It's a real estate contract. "You're buying a house?" I ask him.

"I am."

"You really needed me to look over a real estate contract?" I drop the folder back on the desk.

"There're other documents in there I need you to review," Theo says, pushing the folder towards me again.

Curiosity gets the better of me, so I open the file for a second time and sift through the papers. Estate planning. He's updating his will. "If I sign this, you do know it's legal, right? You walk out that door and find yourself on the wrong end of a bullet and she's going to get everything you have." The attorney in me wants to tell him he's fucking nuts for adding Maddie, a girl he just

117

fucking met, to his will as his sole beneficiary; while the brother in me is hopeful that she's the one who will give him a purpose outside of work. Judging by the fact he's just updated his will and is leaving everything to her, I'd say she already is.

"I'm aware of what it fucking means, Matteo. Just sign it."

"Wait, the cars? Surely Maddie doesn't need the cars. Can't I at least get those?" I pout. Theo stares at me, his eyes squinted in my direction, but doesn't say a word. "I take that as a no then," I say, before signing the documents. Once I've finalized all the changes, I pass the folder across the desk. "Does Pops know about this?"

"Nope."

"Riiiight. Make sure to put him on video call when he learns you're giving everything you have to a girl you're not even dating."

"Fuck off," he grunts.

"Is that why you called me down here? These could have been emailed."

"Tony Gambino, what's happening with the RICO case?"

"He'll be out in a couple of days. The paperwork's been sent to the judge. The whole case is getting thrown out." I smile, thinking how pissed off the Feds are going to be. "Five years of surveillance wasted on a technicality—a fucking loophole."

"They've been on him that long? And how the fuck

did you find a loophole?"

"Yep. I'm more than just a pretty face, big brother. I have brains too."

"Sure you do, but I think it's your little hacker friend down in Beverly Hills who's got the brains," he says without lifting his eyes from his computer screen.

How the fuck does he know about Jasper? "Still, my idea. Just because someone else executed it doesn't make it any less mine." I push to my feet, ready to leave.

"I need you to stop by the warehouse today and do inventory."

I look down at my Armani suit and groan. "You couldn't have told me that before I left the house. Do you have any idea what this jacket is worth?"

"Stop at a fucking store first. I don't give a shit. Just get it fucking done."

"So, are you planning on bringing the new Missus to Christmas in Canada?" I ask him as I make my way to the door.

"Hey, Matteo?" Theo calls out when my open palm lands on the handle.

"Yeah?"

"How was your weekend with Savvy?" He smirks. Fuck, he doesn't know. There's no way anyone could know I got fucking hitched.

"Fine." I turn and walk out the door. I might not be giving her the divorce she thinks she wants, but I'm not ready for the family to know about our nuptials just yet either.

17

SAVVY

There is no fear in love.

1 John 4:18 (ESV)

I'm racking my brain for a way to ditch Rocco. No matter what I've tried, he won't leave my side. Even as I sit behind my desk in my office, he stands guard at my damn door. I had Kirstin, my assistant, try to distract him with her charms while I snuck around the corner. It didn't work. The moment I took one step across the threshold, Rocco's head snapped in my direction. I smiled and faked that I needed a coffee break, despite the fact we both knew I had a steaming-hot cup sitting on my desk already.

I'm not giving up just yet. I will find a way to ditch him if it kills me. This isn't the first time Matteo has sicced one of his guard dogs on me. It never bothered me before, but now I'm annoyed. Probably because, at the moment, I want to run. My feet are itching to get as far away from Matteo as I can. I can't think straight when he's around. I feel like an addict. After one night with him, I can't get enough.

How is it that even sex with Matteo seems so natural? It's like our bodies know each other—even though, other than that one time when we were fifteen, we've never so much as kissed.

Now, my lips tingle at the memory of having his mouth on mine. Kirstin pops her head in my office. "Savannah, you have a three fifteen with Loch Nielson."

"Here?" I ask.

"No, he wants you to meet him at some store. I've sent the details to your phone."

"Great, just what I need, to spend hours in some gaudy store designing the world's ugliest apartment in New York history," I groan, shutting down my laptop.

"I know, but he's paying a handsome fee to have you design that ugly apartment." She laughs.

"Unfortunately, it's his connections I'm more interested in. He's the rising star in the tech world, and all those nerds are clueless when it comes to interior design. That's a pool of potential clients." I stand, straighten my skirt, and walk around the desk.

I might have forced Rocco to make a quick stop at Valentino on the way here this morning. I might have also swiped that emergency black card Matteo insisted I take years ago. I'm surprised the thing actually worked, to be honest. But I did get a little thrill at spending his money, even though my twenty-thousand-dollar shopping spree won't even put a dent in his bank balance.

"Okay, I won't be back in today. I'll see you tomorrow," I tell my assistant.

"Will the silent hunk be joining us again? Oh! Or what about his hot boss?" Kirstin asks.

I look towards Rocco and see his lips tip up. He's doing his best not to smile at Kirstin's less-than-professional commentary. "One, he's not that hunky. Two, his boss is an ass and not welcome in this building." I walk out of my office and head straight for the elevator. Changing my mind at the last minute, I pivot and decide to use the stairs. Or better yet, make Rocco suffer by using the stairs.

It takes me ten minutes to descend the full fifteen flights. My plan to make Rocco suffer backfired, seeing as I'm the only one suffering. Me and my poor feet in these new shoes. Rocco told me more than once I should take them off. I quickly dismissed that suggestion. This is New York City. My office might be in a nice neighborhood, but I'm not about to walk around barefoot.

I finally sink into the back of the SUV and sigh in

relief. Maybe having Rocco drive me around isn't so bad after all. He's just saved me a trip on the subway. I give my hired bodyguard the address of the store, sit back, and relax into the soft interior. I *try* to relax at least. My brain is working overtime as I attempt to figure a way out of this marriage without destroying my friendship. I can feel my lady parts whining in protest at the thought of never having Matteo's skilled hands, mouth, and *other* anatomy touch them. Damn him and his mind-altering orgasms.

"Ma'am, we're here. I'm going to need you to wait in the car a moment though." Rocco's tone is different. Not as easygoing. More serious than I'm used to hearing it.

"Why?" I ask, peering out the window. I don't know what I'm expecting to see, but it looks like a normal New York City sidewalk.

"Ah, this is Russian territory, ma'am. We really shouldn't be here," he says.

"We?"

"The Valentino family, we shouldn't be here. I should have known by the address. I'm sorry, ma'am."

"Look, I get it. You're trying to do your job, but so am I. I have to meet a client in that store right there." I attempt to open the door but it doesn't budge. "Unlock the door, Rocco."

"I can't. Boss's orders. We just have to wait."

"Wait for what? I'm going to be late if I don't go in there," I scream.

"He won't be long."

"Who won't be long? Oh god, you called Matteo, didn't you? Damn it, Rocco," I growl, as my hand fists around my phone. I should call Matteo myself, give him a piece of my mind. Instead, I come up with a better plan. I send Loch Nielson a message.

ME:

> I'm here. I'm having car issues. Any idea how to unlock a car door from the inside?

He sends back a message near instantly.

LOCH NIELSON:

> Yes, I can hack into the vehicle and unlock it for you. I just need the make, model, and license plate number.

"Ah, Rocco, what's the license plate on this car? Is it the same as all the others?" I ask, aware that most of the Valentino vehicles have the license plate *Valentino* followed by a number.

"Um, yeah, why?" he questions me skeptically.

"No reason. What number car is this one? Two hundred?"

"Five."

I send all the info to Loch and then I wait. Maybe he's not that tech savvy, but it was worth a try. Two minutes later, a message comes through.

LOCH NIELSON:

It's done. Try the door now.

I pick up my bag, drop my phone inside, and try the door handle again. To my surprise, it works. I can hear Rocco cursing behind me as I slam the door and high-tail it into the store. "Thanks for that, Loch. You're a lifesaver. So sorry I'm late." I give him my best smile, which he doesn't return. He looks passed me and his face pales.

"Ah, Miss St. James, are you in some kind of trouble?" he asks me.

I glance over my shoulder and lock eyes with one very pissed-off bodyguard, a hand resting on the inside of his jacket. "Nope, I'm good. Just ignore him. Trust me, his bark is way worse than his bite," I say.

"Yeah, somehow I doubt that," Loch replies.

"What are we looking for here? I've never been to this store before." I scan my surroundings and cringe at the god-awful décor.

"I thought you could help me pick out a bed." Loch points to the rows of furniture displayed at the back of the store."

"Main bedroom or guest room?" I ask.

"Main."

"Okay, let's do this." I lead the way, ignoring Rocco's gaze now burning into the back of my neck.

Ten minutes, that's how long I've been listening to Loch drone on about why each bed won't suit his needs. And he's been explicit—some things you really can't unhear. It's also how long it took *him* to get here. I knew he'd come and I sensed him the moment he walked through the door. It's like the air in the place changed. I don't turn around. I don't acknowledge that I know he's here. I keep my attention on my client, even if I want to shake the kid and tell him his taste in furniture is awful.

"Ah, what about this one. Its clean lines are modern but the little curves on the poles give it that antique look you're going for?" I point to a four-poster bed.

"Mmm, you're good, Miss St. James. Sold. I'll take that one."

"Mrs. Valentino." A voice rumbles from right behind me. Loch's eyes widen as he takes in Matteo.

As subtly as I can, I shove an elbow into Matteo's stomach before stepping to the side. "Actually, it's still Miss St. James. What are you doing here, Matteo? I'm working."

"Yeah, I can see that," he grits out. "We need to leave. Now, Savvy."

"What? I can't. I'm not done yet."

"Ah, we're finished here, Miss St…" Loch shuts his mouth when Matteo growls.

"I'm Matteo Valentino. Savvy's husband." He holds out his palm to my client.

I watch as Loch's hand trembles when he brings it up to shake Matteo's. "Loch Nielson."

"I know who you are," Matteo says.

"Loch, I'm really sorry about this. How about we

reschedule for tomorrow? I can clear my calendar and we can go over the other bedrooms."

"Ah, sure, whatever you want." Loch turns around and heads for the door.

"Mr. Nielson," Matteo calls out.

"Yes?"

"Hack into one of my cars again and you won't be walking out of anywhere. Ever."

I gasp. Matteo *did not* just threaten to kill my client.

"Ah, sure, sorry, sir. Won't happen again."

"I'm actually going to kill you. For real this time, Matteo. How dare you?" My arms fold over my chest.

"How dare I? How fucking dare I?" Matteo closes in on me, pressing my back against the edge of a dresser. "Rocco, lock the door. Make sure no one gets in."

"Sure, boss."

I hear Rocco leave, and when I look around, I notice that the whole store is empty and there's a wall of men in black suits stationed along the front of the building. "Matteo, what's going on?" I ask.

"You're in fucking Russian territory, Savvy. You can't just come to this neighborhood and expect to walk out in one piece. Whether you like it or not, you're a fucking Valentino. A fact that's not going to change."

"Oh, it's changing," I tell him. My eyes travel up and down his body. He's disheveled, visibly distressed. And that's not like Matteo at all, is it?

"Oh my god, are you hurt? What the hell, Matteo?" I

reach out to open his jacket, so I can see where the blood covering his shirt is coming from.

Matteo's hand snatches my wrist midair before I can even make contact. "I'm fine. It's not my blood, Savvy. Come on, I need to get you out of here."

18

MATTEO

"Rouse him, and learn the principle of his activity or inactivity. Force him to reveal himself, so as to find out his vulnerable spots."

— **Sun Tzu, The Art of War**

I could wring her pretty little neck for being so reckless. And that little shit who hacked into my car's system to unlock the door for her? Yeah, he's lucky he's still fucking breathing. Let alone standing upright. I pull Savvy towards the door and stop dead in my tracks when I hear the first gunshot.

"Fuck." I turn around and push her towards the back of the store. I know my men out front can handle themselves. My main priority right now is to get Savvy out of here as quickly as I can. When we reach the back door, I remove two guns from my covert holsters, handing one over to her. I know she knows how to use it, because I fucking taught her to shoot when we were teenagers. "Remember: shoot first, ask questions later," I remind her.

She nods, her complexion pale and her eyes full of fear. It's a look I never fucking want to see on her face.

"Just stay behind me. If I tell you to run, fucking run and don't stop."

"Matteo, what's happening?"

"The Russians don't seem to like us being here too much. It's fine. Just a little misunderstanding, babe. Come on." Pushing the back door open, I look up and down the alleyway. It's quiet, empty. I take Savvy's hand and make a run for it, leading her to the other end. We reach the back street just as a car screeches to a stop right in front of us. I breathe a sigh of relief at seeing one of my men. Opening the back door, I practically lift Savvy up and throw her inside. "Make sure she gets home, Rocco."

"What? No! Matteo, get in the damn car right now!" Savvy reaches out to me, her hands clinging to my shirt.

Untangling her fingers from my chest, I lean in, giving her a quick peck on the lips. "I'll be there before you know it, babe. I have work to finish." I shut the door on her. I can hear her screaming, banging on the window, but I can't give in to her right now. She's safe. Rocco will get her home.

Rushing back down the alleyway, I pause at the storefront and stare at the resulting bloodbath. There's three Russians laid out in the middle of the goddamn street. One of my men is leaning against the wall, a palm pressed to his shoulder.

"Get him to a medic," I order the soldier to my left. "You three, get this shit cleaned up. And, Joey, catch up with Rocco. Ensure that car gets home unscathed." I look at the mess on the street. Running my fingers through my hair, I make the call I really hate fucking making.

He answers on the second ring—fucker probably already knows what just went down. "Matteo, are you bleeding?" he says in greeting.

"No, Pops, but thanks for your concern." I smirk, knowing that's not why he's asking.

"Good, then get your fucking ass to the warehouse, finish that inventory, and then drop by and see me so you can explain why you had to start a fucking shootout with the Russians on a goddamn Monday afternoon." He hangs up the phone.

I drag a hand down my face. How is it that a day that started out so fucking good could turn into such a shitshow?

I nod my head at the only two soldiers left without

an assigned task. They follow me to my car. I climb in the back while my men jump in the front. "Where to, boss?" Christian, a new recruit, asks.

"The warehouse. It's going to be a fucking long night, boys." I groan, wishing I had just got in the car with Savvy and driven away. I really need to get out of this fucking city for a bit. That trip to Australia I told my mom I was taking—yeah, that needs to fucking happen.

It takes twenty minutes in gridlock traffic to get back to the warehouse. Before I go inside, I send a message to Rocco.

ME:

Let me know when you make it home.

I get a reply instantly.

ROCCO:

Sure thing, boss.

I'm tempted to ask how she is but decide against it. I don't need to ask. I know she's going to be pissed as all hell.

I walk into the warehouse, whistling the tune of "Red Right Hand" by Nick Cave and The Bad Seeds, my fists flexing open and closed. I'm pumped to finish what I started before I was called away to get my wife out of fucking enemy territory. Although no one knows she's my wife, everyone has seen Savvy and me together enough in the press to know she's important to me. And our enemies aren't above using her to their advantage. It'd be the last fucking thing they ever did, but that wouldn't stop the fuckers from trying.

The guy who's currently on my family's inventory list is Cillian McGregor, a low-level IRA member. Our boys found him lurking around one of our shipping containers on the port. That being said, he's too insignificant to be out here working alone. I'll give the little shit credit. He hasn't broken yet. He will though; they always do. I just have to find the right method to break him.

He looks up and smiles at me. As much as I want to swing a fist and wipe that smirk off his face, I've tried that. It didn't fucking work. It's time for a different tactic. Sitting down in the chair opposite him, I take my phone out and call the doc.

"Hello."

"Hey, Doc, I'm going to need you to meet me at the warehouse with enough bags of plasma to keep a little fucker from bleeding out as I cut his limbs off, one by fucking one."

"Ah, sure, I'll see what I can do."

"You do that. See you when you get here." I hang up and stare at the little redheaded fucker in front of me. "You're good, but you're not that good." Leaning back in my chair, I tip my head to one of the soldiers, and he brings me a bag of cutting implements, dropping it at my feet. I quickly reach in and find what I'm looking for—the reciprocating saw—before drawing it out. "This is all I'm gonna need."

"Feck you. Do ya worst. I ain't tellin' ya shit," he spits out between broken teeth.

I gotta admit his accent does bring a smile to my face. Even angry, these idiots have a way of sounding happy. I think it has something to do with their pronunciation of words. I look over to the new guy and ask, "Hey, Christian, how many of them say that?"

"All of 'em, boss." Christian smirks.

"And how many of them make it through without giving me what I want," I continue.

"Not a single fucking one, boss," Christian confirms.

"That's right, not a single fucking one." I push to my feet, placing the saw on the ground in front of me. Then I remove my jacket and set it over the back of the chair before I proceed to roll the sleeves of my dress shirt up to my elbows. You'd think I'd learn by now that I need to carry a spare set of clothes with me every day. In this job, I never fucking know what I'll be doing, how messy I'll be making things.

Most days, I'm stuck sitting in an office building, staring at endless piles of paperwork. But it's days like this, days where I actually have to get my hands dirty, that I enjoy my chosen profession way more than I'll admit. There's a reason I'm the one here, doing this, and not one of my other brothers, or one of our men. I'm fucking good at it. I could spend hours inflicting pain on someone and still sleep like a damn baby at night.

I remove my Rolex from my wrist—Pops gave each of us the same watch for our twenty-first birthday. The one time I didn't take it off, I ended up having to send the damn thing away to be cleaned. And let me tell you, nothing is worth sitting through another lecture about how stupid I was that day.

"In about five minutes, the doc will be here. That's when we'll start this party," I announce, passing my Rolex to Christian.

"Can't fucking wait," he says. I like this recruit. I've known him since we were kids. His father is one of our capos. I never thought Christian would follow this path. I'm fucking glad he has though. He's smart, quick, and not the least bit squeamish.

❦

ONE FOOT AND TWO HANDS. The amputated limbs sit in a pile on the floor on top of a tarp. "Who sent you?" I ask again, for the tenth time.

"Ye mam, after I left her bed this morning." He screams through the pain of me cauterizing his open wound with the blowtorch.

My fist connects with the left side of his temple. "Wrong fucking answer." I hold out a palm to Christian, and he places the reciprocating saw in my grasp. "What should I take next? Your one remaining foot? An elbow?"

"Feck off!" Cillian spits. "I don't know whatcha want me to fuckin' tell ye."

"I want to know why the fuck you're snooping around our docks, and who the fuck sent you."

"They'll kill me," he says.

I smile. He's coming around. They always do. Eventually. "You're a dead man anyway, Cillian. It's up to you if you want to die slowly, piece by fucking piece. *Or* you can tell me what I want to know and I'll show you some mercy."

I see the look in his eyes. The one that says he's going to give in. That he finally realizes he's not getting out of here alive. That no one is coming to rescue his ass. "It's the Russians. They paid me to blow up a few containers. That's it. I swear it," he cries out.

"The Russians? What Russians?" I ask, hitting the button on the saw—it comes to life with an ominous sound.

"Fuck, I don't know. Some fucker by the name of Petrov. I swear I don't know nothin' else."

Moving closer with the power tool, I lower it to just above his elbow. "Thanks. That wasn't so hard, was it?" I ask, right before the saw makes contact with his skin.

"Ahh, stop. I told ye. You said... you said mercy... fuck!" he screams.

"There's something you should know about me. Mercy is granted by weak men. And I'm not fucking weak. I'm merciless."

19

SAVVY

Do not make friends with a hot-tempered person, do not associate with one easily angered, or you may learn their ways and get yourself ensnared.

Proverbs 22:24-25

I often wonder what my life would have turned out like if I'd listened to my father all those years ago and stayed far away from Matteo. At the time, I thought my father was just a controlling, overbearing parental figure.

Now, I know better. He knew—of course, he knew what would happen if I let myself be ensnared by the world the Valentino's inhabit. Although, I do question why he didn't fight harder to get me away from them...

Sometimes I wish he just packed us up and moved across the country when my mother died. Not that I would doubt for a minute that even a twelve-year-old Matteo would have found a way to hunt me down. He's always been resourceful.

Why? It's the one word repeating through my mind right now. Why didn't he just get in the car with me? Why did I have to prove a point and go into the store, even though I knew Rocco's concerns were valid? Why do I feel guilty for doing my damn job? Why am I sitting on the floor of an empty living room with dread pooling in the pit of my stomach? Why am I waiting for him to come home? If he isn't already dead in a ditch somewhere...

No, he isn't. I would know by now if he were. Wouldn't I? I have to believe the loss of the other half of your soul would hurt a hell of a lot more than what I'm feeling right now. That knowledge doesn't stop the worry. Maybe I should call him, send him a message just to check that his heart is still beating.

I can't do it. As much as I want to, my rage is warring with my concern.

I look up when I see Rocco walk past the doorway to the living room for the hundredth time. He stares into the darkness but doesn't say anything. He knows I'm here. It's not like I've been quiet while cursing out

Matteo to the empty space. I stopped yelling into the void when guilt took over.

What if that was it? The last time I'll ever get to see him. What if it's me who ends up getting him killed? My stubbornness. My actions. Then the question I've asked myself a million times over the past year pops into my mind. Can I really ever see myself living a life without Matteo in it?

The answer is no.

But the other question remains as well. Can I live this life with Matteo? Can I be the dutiful wife who waits at home, wondering if her husband is going to make it back? Wondering if the enemy is going to storm the house and find her? Use her against him?

Again, the answer is no.

I don't have a solution. I wish God would send me a sign, tell me what I'm supposed to do here. It's not supposed to be this hard. In the movies or books, they make it seem easy. You find your soul mate, fall head over heels, overcome a little problem, and live happily ever after.

My problem isn't little though; it's been festering for years. And it's not really something Matteo can help me out with. It's up to me to overcome it. If I can, does that mean I'll get my happily ever after with Matteo? Who knows.

However, I do think I should at least try. I just wish I had someone to talk to, someone to give me advice on how I can overcome these insecurities and fears I have. I probably need to see a shrink. But what do I even say? That my head's messed up because my best friend, who I've been in love with for forever, married me in Vegas. Which is great, apart from the fact that he's a goddamn mafia prince and chances are I'll be left alone and heartbroken. No, not heartbroken, soul-broken, just like my dad after my mom died.

Yeah, I don't see that working out in my favor. I can't tell anyone about Matteo's family. Not that everyone doesn't already know—it's speculated. The rumors spread like wildfire through the streets of New York, but it's not discussed by the family to outsiders.

Rocco walks past the doorway, peers in, and again doesn't say anything. Pushing to my feet, I decide that enough is enough. I'm not going to sit here and feel sorry for myself when I can be in a perfectly comfy bed upstairs... also feeling sorry for myself.

I make it to the top landing when the front door opens and Matteo walks in. He stops when he looks up and sees me. The tension between the two of us is palpable as we both stand frozen, staring at each other.

After what seems like hours, but is most likely minutes, Rocco appears, breaking whatever hold Matteo's gaze had on me. I turn and storm into the bedroom, slamming and locking the door behind me. All thoughts of trying to let go of these hang-ups have just flown out the window. I don't even want to see him right now. The worry and fear that he wouldn't come home evaporated when he walked through the door. Then it was replaced by rage and relief.

I'm holding on to the rage. It's irrational, how I was scared I wouldn't see him again, and yet all I want to do is strangle the life out of him for making me worry like that.

Before I make it to the shower, the handle on the bedroom rattles and loud banging echoes through the enclosed space. "Savvy, open the door," Matteo yells through the barrier.

Ignoring him, I turn the water on. He can sleep on the kitchen tiles for all I care. The sound from the shower muffles Matteo's shouts. I strip out of my clothes and step under the stream. I close my eyes and let the hot water fall over my face.

I don't hear him enter the bathroom, but I know he's here. I can feel him. Feel his eyes on me. "I have nothing to say to you right now, Matteo."

"Good, then maybe you'll listen to what I have to say to you." He slips off his shoes before stepping into the glass cubicle.

"Wh-what are you doing?" I ask, stepping back.

"What you did today was fucking stupid and reckless, Savvy." His words are harsh, his tone even harsher. I'm not used to this side of Matteo being directed at me.

"No, what you did today was fucking stupid and reckless, Matteo." I shove at his chest but he doesn't budge. Not even an inch. Pulling my fingertips away, I look down. That's when I see how much blood coats his shirt. It's not the first time I've seen him like this and it probably won't be the last.

"I'm fine, Savvy. Not a scratch on me." He smirks.

"I'm glad you're okay," I tell him. I really am. "But I'm not. I can't do this, Matteo. Please don't make me do this."

I see the hurt in his eyes. "Do what?" he asks.

"I can't sit at home every night, wondering where you are, not knowing if you're going to come back. Thinking that you're... I can't handle the thought of not seeing you again."

"I will always come home to you, Savvy."

"Ten hours, Matteo. You shoved me into the back of a car and ran off to do God knows what. I haven't heard from you for ten hours. That's how long I sat here, wondering if you were already dead. I can't live like this. I can't."

"I'm sorry I didn't call. I was working."

"Working? Right. Well, while you were working, I was going out of my damn mind." I yank my hands free, and this time he lets me.

"Savvy, what is it that you want, exactly?" Matteo questions suddenly.

My eyes linger on the fact that he's undoing his now soaking-wet shirt. Inch by inch, more of that delicious, tanned skin is revealed. Nope, not getting distracted by his damn body. "I want a divorce," I tell him for what feels like the hundredth time.

"And I've told you you're never getting one. So we," he says, pointing between the two of us, "need to come up with a compromise. A way to make this work. Because, for better or worse, you are my wife, Savannah, and I won't be doing a damn thing to change that."

Turning my back to him, I pick up the bodywash, squirting it into my hands before I scrub them clean.

"Savvy, I love you," Matteo says when I step out of the shower and wrap a towel around myself.

I turn back to face him. "I love you too. That's the problem, Matteo. Because I know that this love will consume me if I let it, and what will be left of me when you're not around anymore?"

Matteo opens and closes his mouth, but he doesn't say anything. And I walk out of the bathroom, softly shutting the door behind me.

20

MATTEO

In the midst of chaos, there is also opportunity.

– Sun Tzu, The Art of War

Savvy's words had me speechless. I knew she had hang-ups about us being together. I just didn't realize how deep they went. Even after she'd told me how she was afraid of losing me this morning, I didn't think…

I'm such a fucking idiot. I should have taken the time to call or message her throughout the night. My stomach twists at the thought of her sitting here worrying about me like that. I don't want that for her any more than she does. I just don't know how the fuck I'm supposed to reassure her that I'm not planning on going anywhere. I just need to be better at making sure she knows I'm not laid out cold somewhere with a bullet stuck between my eyes.

By the time I've finished up in the shower, Savvy is lying in bed pretending to be asleep already. Avoidance, that's what she's going for. I drag on a pair of sweats and head downstairs. She might be able to resist me after years of practice, but I know she can't resist vanilla ice cream with fresh strawberries and chocolate sauce.

I bring the bowl back upstairs to the bedroom. And, making as much noise as I can, I flip on the bedside lights before I slip under the covers next to her. I feel her body stiffen but she doesn't turn around. Picking up the remote, I press a button to bring the television down from the ceiling. The noise of the motor has Savvy rolling over and looking up.

"There's a television in here? I spent all afternoon in an empty house and you've had a television hidden in the ceiling?" she huffs.

"You could have asked. And I would have told you." I flick through to Hulu and turn on the latest episode of *Yellowstone*. I know Savvy loves this show. Throwing the remote down on the table, I pick up the bowl and scoop a spoonful of ice cream and strawberries before holding it in front of my mouth for a moment. I can feel Savvy's eyes on me. On my spoon. I turn my head to face her, raising one eyebrow in question. "Are you okay?" I ask.

"You're playing really dirty, Matteo, even for you." She smiles.

I sink the spoon into my mouth and moan as loud as I can. "I have no idea what you're talking about, babe," I say between bites.

"If you don't hand that bowl over in the next two minutes, you best be sleeping with one eye open, because I *will* murder you," she says.

I point the now-empty spoon in her direction. "You know that threat would have been scarier if you hadn't just confessed your undying love for me."

"What? I didn't," she argues.

"Yeah, you did." I can't keep the smile off my face. "But here, you can have my ice cream. Because that's the kind of husband I am, Savvy. The one who gives you the last bowl of ice cream. You really did hit the jackpot when you locked me down."

"You're a moron. Give it." She snatches the bowl and spoon from me.

I watch as her eyes close with the first taste. My dick hardens instantly, as much as I want to throw that bowl away and bury myself inside her, we need to talk this shit out. "My mom wants to know if you're coming to Canada for Christmas next week." Yep, I'm good at talking about anything but the real issue.

Savvy eyes me warily. "I can't go to Canada with your family, Matteo."

"Why the fuck not? You spend Christmas with us every year." I frown.

"That was before we got drunk married and you refused to give me divorce papers," she says.

"You know my family will have a hissy fit if I miss Christmas. We have to go."

"No, *you* have to go. I don't. I'm not stopping you from going to Canada, Matteo."

"And I'm not spending our first Christmas as a married couple without you. So, if you don't want to go, we'll stay here. Do Christmas just the two of us." She's out of her mind if she thinks I'll leave her behind. I wouldn't have done that when we were friends. I sure as shit won't do it now that she's my wife.

"You can't *not* be with your family for Christmas, Matteo. Also, your mother will hate me if she finds out you didn't go because of me," Savvy says as she shoves another spoonful of ice cream into her mouth.

"First, *you* are my family, Savvy. The most important part of it. Second, my mother could never hate you." I often wonder if my mother loves Savvy more than me. Whenever Savannah is over at the house, or attending family gatherings, she gets the preferential treatment from mom, not me or any one of my brothers.

"She will, when she finds out I want a divorce from her precious baby boy."

"Wanting and getting are two different things. And, besides, we don't have to tell them yet. If that will make you more comfortable, we can go spend Christmas in Canada and pretend that we're nothing more than just best friends." I smirk and then add, "It's not like we haven't been pretending for years anyway."

"We *have been* nothing more than best friends. And you know what the shitty part of all this is?" Savvy asks.

"What?"

"Today, when I was scared, angry, confused... all I wanted to do was call and ask you for advice. And then I wanted to call your mom and ask her instead. But I couldn't do either of those things. The two people I can usually talk my problems through with, I couldn't."

I sit up and cross my legs over, facing her fully. "Savannah, you can always call me. I don't care what time of day it is, what I'm doing, I will always make time for you."

We've never *not* talked to each other about shit, and I don't want that to change now. Was she right all these years? Has getting married already destroyed the friendship we had?

I won't let it. We can have both.

"I can't talk to you about this, Matteo. You seem dead set on keeping this marriage thing going, whereas I'm certain it's a mistake. It's going to ruin us."

"Tell me one thing? Tell me you don't love me. Look me in the eye and tell me you're not in love with me."

She lifts her eyes to meet mine. I can see the indecision on her face. She's considering lying to me. But then she doesn't. "I can't. You know that. But love isn't enough."

"Love is all we need, babe. You and me, we are unbreakable. Always have been. Being married, that only makes our bond stronger. Not weaker."

"You don't know how scared I was today, Tao. I've always worried about you, always. But today, it was more than just worry. That fear was something I don't want to feel again."

"I do know, actually. When Rocco told me where you were and that you just waltzed into a fucking store in the middle of Russian territory, I was scared. There's not much that scares me in this life, Savvy. But losing you is at the top of that list. I get it, but we are not going to let fear stop us from living the life we both know we want."

"What else is on your list? Spiders? Snakes? Bears?"

I let her change the topic. I know if I push her too much right now, she'll just run out the door. Or at least try to. "Under losing you is something happening to Theo."

Her eyebrows raise. "Just Theo, and not the twins?"

"I'm the spare, Savvy. I like being the spare. I don't ever want to be the heir. That job is all his." I know I shouldn't have brought it up. This is what terrifies her, my family's business. "Hey, after Christmas, we're going to Melbourne for a few weeks."

"Melbourne? Why? And I can't just up and go. I have a job, an office to run."

"Take time off. I have some business to do there and I don't want to go without you."

"What business?" she asks.

I'm thrown by her question. She never usually asks about my business or what I do. I know she doesn't want to know. I also don't want her to know. If Savvy saw what I was actually capable of, what I do to another human without so much as batting an eye, I don't think she'd ever look at me the same. I know she's not stupid. Tonight isn't the first time she's seen me come home covered in someone else's blood. But knowing and seeing are different things.

"I... uh... fine. It's not entirely business related. My cousin and her idiot husband are relocating to Melbourne for a while or something. I don't want Hope there alone."

"Matteo, she's not alone. You said it yourself: she'll be with her husband."

"Who's an idiot," I remind her.

"An idiot who, if I remember hearing the story correctly, put you on your ass." She laughs.

The son of a bitch *did* knock me out cold last year. We all went over to Sydney when we heard Lily, our nightmare twin cousin number two, was shacking up with her now-husband—Alex. To say we didn't approve of the relationship is putting it lightly.

Hope went missing during our visit—except we later determined she wasn't missing at all. She was hooking up with her cousin Ash's best friend, Chase. When I saw her in that bed, my mind went back to when she was sixteen and my brother and I walked up on some fucker raping her. That's not something I could ever forget. I may have overreacted and wanted to put a bullet through Chase's head. Still fucking do. That fucker is lucky Hope loves him so damn much. If it weren't for her, I would have had him in a million pieces before feeding him to the sharks in the fucking Sydney Harbor.

"You're supposed to be on my side here. Besides, he got a lucky shot in. That's all."

"How long will we be gone?" she asks.

"I'm not sure. Why?"

"I have a business too, Matteo. I'm not your trophy wife."

"But damn would you make a good one." My eyes roam up and down her body. She's wearing a black t-shirt of mine. I can see her nipples poking through the fabric.

"I'm serious, Tao. How long will I need to be gone?"

"A few weeks, tops."

"Okay."

"Okay, you'll come to Australia?"

"Let's not pretend you were actually giving me a choice. I wouldn't put it past you to handcuff us together again and drag me kicking and screaming onto the Valentino jet."

Ignoring that statement, because the thought did actually cross my mind, I ask, "And Christmas, should I tell my mom you'll be there too?"

"If I come, we can't tell anyone about this," she says, pointing between the two of us.

"I'm fine with that."

"So, those papers?"

"Never fucking happening, Savannah," I growl. "We will work this out. We'll be fine."

"Thanks for the ice cream." She hands the empty bowl back to me. "Let's just watch the show and worry about tomorrow, tomorrow."

"Sounds like a good idea," I agree, placing the bowl on the nightstand. I flick the light off and lie down. It doesn't take long for Savvy to crawl over next to me. She rests her head on my chest, and my arm wraps around her back.

This feels right. Having her here in my arms is right.

21

SAVVY

Do everything in love.

— Corinthians 16:14

I like Matteo's family. I've always loved being around them and have never once felt like I shouldn't be here. Until now.

Guilt is eating at me. I'm lying. *We're* lying. Matteo, he does it so well. He's used to playing whatever persona is expected of him at any given event. For me, it doesn't come so easily. Matteo's been leaving my bed every morning at the crack of dawn before anyone wakes.

Oh yeah, that's another thing I'm lying about. Well, at least to myself. I'm addicted to him. To his touch, to the pleasure he wrings from my body. How did I go all these years resisting him?

Whatever strength I had that made it possible to resist his touch flew out the damn window with the first ten orgasms he gave me. But I'm still in denial. I can stop at any time, right? When we go back to just being friends, I'll survive. I think. Although, the longer I spend with Matteo in this new dynamic, the more I'm struggling with the idea of giving it up.

"Savannah, let's go for a walk," Holly calls out to me in her *don't even think about arguing with my request* tone. Shit, that tone's usually reserved for the boys. I look to Romeo and Luca, who are sitting on the sofa opposite me bickering about something. They pause mid-insult at the sound of their mother's voice and their eyes widen at me.

"Oooooh, Savannah's in trouble…" they sing out at the same time.

"Ignore them, Savannah," Holly says with a flick of her wrist, then steps in front of her youngest sons, shaking her head at them. "I wonder where I went wrong sometimes."

"Ah, Ma, 4.0 GPA sitting right here." Romeo smirks —an expression all four Valentino brothers seem to have mastered. Although none of them have the same effect Matteo has on me.

"And yet it seems we're paying for extra tutoring sessions, Romeo." Holly laughs. The twins sober up, their lips sealed tight as they share a look with each other. "I'll deal with that can of worms later. Savannah, come on." Holly starts walking towards the front of the house.

Standing, I give the boys a questioning eyebrow. Why does Romeo need a tutor? I swear he's the smartest of them all. Then it clicks. "It's a girl, isn't it?" I ask him before exiting the room.

His answering scoff tells me everything. It seems our little Romeo has found himself a Juliet. I laugh, quickening my stride to catch up to Holly. There's a line of coats hanging from the hooks by the front door. I grab mine and slide my feet into a pair of boots before finding Holly waiting for me at the bottom of the front steps.

"Okay, am I actually in trouble?" I ask her nervously. Matteo's mother may seem like the sweet innocent kind, but I have no doubt that she's just as ruthless as her husband when she deems it necessary.

Holly scrutinizes me. It feels like her gaze is peering right into my soul. "No, you're not in trouble, Savannah. What makes you think that you are? Have you done something I don't know about?"

Shit, she knows. How can she know? Surely Matteo wouldn't have told her. No, he would have told me if he had. "Uh…" I'm at a loss for words.

"Relax, come on. Whatever it is that's eating at you, we can work it out," she says with such confidence.

"I'm not sure this can be worked out so well," I tell her.

"Anything can be worked out, Savannah."

The cold stings my face as we stroll down the path in silence for a while. This property feels like it's in the middle of nowhere; it's more like a compound surrounded by armed guards. It's the kind of place where you can feel alone in an open space—though, in truth, you're never really alone. Not here. Not with everyone watching.

"Okay, spit it out, before we both freeze to death out here," Holly says.

"I... uh... I have this friend who did something I never thought she'd do," I lie.

"And what is it that this *friend* did?" she asks, emphasizing the word *friend*.

"She went to Vegas for a weekend with another friend and married him. Now she doesn't know what to do."

"Does she love him? This friend she married," Holly probes, after a beat of silence.

"More than anything," I answer truthfully.

"Does he love her?"

"I have no doubt that he does."

"Then I'm not really seeing your friend's problem."

"I think she's scared. Of ruining the friendship, of losing him. His job is... dangerous and she scared it's going to take him away from her."

"Well, as a wife to someone who has a dangerous job, I would tell your friend not to dwell on the *what ifs* and live for the moment. For today." Holly's advice is reasonable.

"How do you do it? You always seem so calm and relaxed. How do you not live in a state of constant worry?" I ask her.

"Oh, I do—believe me. You know, when I first met Theo, I was scared that his, ah, lifestyle would take him away from me. And one day it might, but I wouldn't give him up for anything. Certainly not fear."

"Mmm, you're a one-of-a-kind kind of woman, Holly. Mr. Valentino is lucky to have you."

"He is," Holly agrees, laughing as she does so. We turn around and walk back to the house. Just before we reach the steps, Holly's hand reaches out to stop me. Pulling me against her, she wraps her arms around me. "Whatever happens, Savannah, you will always be part of this family. No matter what. I would be delighted to keep you as a daughter-in-law though," she whispers into my ear.

I'm speechless as I watch Holly walk away. She knew all along I was talking about us. About her son and me. As soon as I enter the house, I send Matteo a message.

ME:

My bedroom, now!

He doesn't respond, but by the time I'm walking into the bedroom, he's right behind me with that smoldering smirk on his face. "Babe, are we really at the stage where we're demanding booty calls via text messages? 'Cause I gotta say… *I'm totally down for it.*" His grin widens with his suggestive tone.

"Shh!" I pull him into the room. "This is serious, Tao. It's not funny."

"What happened?" he asks, the jovial attitude wiped off his face near instantly.

"Your mom knows," I hiss as I start pacing the room.

"What do you mean *she knows*? What does she know?" Matteo would argue, but he's a big-time momma's boy, so the thought gives him momentary pause. He hates being on his mother's bad side.

"She knows what we did. She knows we got married," I tell him, my arms waving around to further signal my distress.

He smiles—freaking smiles. "Savannah, there is no way she knows. Unless one of us told her, she doesn't know."

"I might have told her."

"Wait… what do you mean you might have told her?"

"Okay, I didn't tell her exactly, but I told her it was my friend. And, obviously, she didn't buy that."

"Fuck! My mom knows? Shit." Now Matteo is the one pacing the room before he suddenly stops to grab me around the waist. "You know what? It doesn't matter. I don't give a shit if the whole world knows you're my wife. In fact, I think everyone should know."

"And what happens when we don't work? When this blows up in our faces?" I ask him.

"I'm not going to let this *not work*, babe. You and me, it's always going to be."

I'm about to tell him he can't know that, that he can't predict the future, when his mouth comes down onto mine. As soon as his tongue delves past my lips, all negative thoughts are replaced with desire—hot, needy desire. Matteo moves us until the back of my legs hit the bed. He pushes on my shoulders, and I fall backwards. I will never tire of the sight of him above me, how his eyes roam over my body so hungrily. Even when I'm fully dressed, it's like he can see right through the fabric.

"You know what this means, right? If people know, we don't have to sneak around this house. I can make you scream my name loud enough for all of Canada to hear."

"We're not letting your family hear us have sex, Matteo. Are you insane?"

"Insanely horny, yes. Insanely in love with you, also yes." His fingers undo the button on my jeans, and before I know it, he's sliding the denim down my legs. "Fottuta bellezza senza sforzo," Matteo says while looking down at me.

Sitting upright, I pull my shirt over my head, reach behind my back, and unclasp my bra. There's no point denying that I want this. That I want him. I swear he's trying to kill me by way of orgasm, but I'm not complaining. Nor am I about to stop his efforts.

I watch as Matteo reaches a hand over the back of his head and pulls his own shirt off in that way men seem to have mastered. I swear, no matter how much I see his body, it's like I'm seeing it for the first time. Every time. My breath hitches. All those hard lines and ridges... That tanned, smooth skin I want to run my tongue over... I want to lick every inch of him declaring "I licked it so it's mine" to anyone within earshot.

That's actually a great idea—one I intend to follow through on right now. My fingers reach out to undo Matteo's belt. I flick his button open and slowly slide the zipper down. Pushing him back a step, I slip off the bed and onto my knees. Looking up at Matteo from this angle has my pussy begging for attention. It really shouldn't be legal for one man to be this sinfully hot.

My hands grip the sides of his jeans, tugging them down along with his boxers. His cock bounces free. My tongue dips out to lick my now-dry lips. Wrapping one hand around his rock-hard shaft, I slide my palm up and down while maintaining eye contact with him.

"Fuck, Savvy, this isn't going to last long if you keep looking at me like that." Matteo's hands cup each side of my face, his thumbs rubbing lightly up and down my cheeks. There is so much love and adoration reflected in his gaze, in his touch, it's almost too much to bear.

My tongue slides out and licks up the underside of his shaft—while those words from earlier repeat on a loop in my head. *I've licked him so he's mine.* And, for once, the idea of Matteo being fully mine doesn't scare me. I don't want to run. No, right now, I have this overwhelming urge to hold on tight and never let him leave my sight. I swirl my tongue around the tip of his cock. The taste of his precum invades my mouth. Closing my lips just around the tip, I suck as my hand pumps up and down the rest of him.

"Fuck, Savannah, I'm going to fucking lose control in a minute here," he hisses.

Releasing his cock from my mouth, I look up at him. "What happens if you lose control, Matteo?" I prompt. I've had a lingering feeling that he's always holding back a little. I don't want him to hold back. I want him to give me everything he has.

"I don't want to lose control with you, Savvy. I don't want to hurt you." His words are whispered, barely audible, but I hear them.

"You could never hurt me Matteo—not like that. I trust you," I tell him.

"Fuck."

And the next thing I know, I'm being picked up and thrown onto the bed. Matteo pulls his jeans and boxers all the way off before jumping on top of me, moving quicker than I've ever seen him move before. He straddles my chest.

His cock—hard, almost angry-looking—is wrapped

in one hand while his other palm closes around my throat. "You're not going to be able to speak when I'm shoving my cock down your throat. So, if it gets to be too much, I want you to tap me twice on the arm."

My eyes widen and my stomach twists in excitement and fear of the newness of this experience. But what has me questioning myself is the fact that my pussy has never been wetter than it is right now while I lie completely helpless, at the mercy of Matteo. A man I know for a fact has never shown anyone mercy.

"I need you to agree, Savvy. Tell me you understand," he grits out between clenched teeth.

"I get it." I nod as much as I can while his hand remains firmly seated around my throat. As soon as the words are out, Matteo squats over my face. And my mouth opens, willingly inviting him in.

I suck him deeper, doing my best not to gag when he hits the back of my throat. "Do not fucking pass out on me, Savvy. I swear to God, if you pass out, we'll be practicing this every day until you learn to fucking stay with me," he says as he pulls his cock out before shoving it back inside again.

My hands grip his ass. It's different from this angle. I'm so out of my depth here but so freaking turned on. My hips are moving upwards, seeking something, and pleasure builds between my legs as Matteo uses my mouth.

"Fuck, your mouth is so fucking perfect," he moans as I suck even harder than I was. I slide one of my hands around and cup his balls, gently massaging them as he thrusts harder. Faster. "Fuck, fuck. Goddamn it," he curses right before I feel warm, salty liquid squirt down my throat. "Lick it clean," Matteo orders and I comply without complaint. When I'm finished, he slides himself down my body, positioning his legs between mine while forcing my thighs to part. "I like seeing you like this, so agreeable. I think you've been so good you deserve a reward, babe."

I nod my head. I want a reward. I really do. And if it's what I think it's going to be, than I need to remember to be more *agreeable* in the future. Although, outside the bedroom, that's hardly going to be our reality.

Matteo stops when he reaches my legs. He grips my black lace panties in his hands and tears them right off my body. Kneeling between my thighs, he spreads them wide open, his finger sliding up my wet folds. "You're fucking drenched, Savvy. You liked that, didn't you? You got off on me choking you with my cock," he asks.

I can't answer. Everything goes hazy as his finger circles my clit. My hips buck upwards, seeking more. I need more. I need something. Matteo's hands move to my ankles, and he rests one on each shoulder before his fingertips glide along the span of my legs, stopping when they reach my hips. I don't know how he does it. But I'm lifted in the air, until just the top of my back and shoulders are on the mattress.

"Again, don't fucking pass out because nothing is going to stop me from enjoying the fuck out of this cunt." Matteo's tongue slides along my slit, and pleasure rings out through my whole body.

I don't think I have to worry about the blood rushing to my head, because I'm so worked up it's not going to take long before I'm flying into orgasmic bliss. Matteo's fingers dig into my hips, no doubt leaving bruises.

"Oh god, Matteo, don't stop." I muffle my moans with my hand, thankful I'm not a total wanton whore who forgets we're in a house filled with his whole extended family.

Matteo works his tongue harder, and his teeth graze my clit right before he starts sucking on it, sending me plummeting off that edge. My legs seize up, clamping around his head. And my back goes rigid as he continues to lick me through my orgasm. Once my body relaxes and I come back down to earth, Matteo slowly lowers me onto the mattress. I lie there, panting for breath.

"Don't think we're anywhere close to being finished here, Savvy. I'm only just getting warmed up." That's the only warning I get before he thrusts his cock into my pussy.

"Oh fuck!" I'm so wet it slides in easily, but that doesn't stop the stretch and slight sting that always comes with Matteo entering me. Not that I'm complaining.

MATTEO

There are roads which must not be followed, armies which must not be attacked, towns which must not be besieged, positions which must not be contested, commands of the sovereign which must not be obeyed.

– Sun Tzu, The Art of War

Theo leaves in a few hours to head back to New York. He won't say why he's going, but I already know it has something to do with Maddie. The girl he's been stalking, obsessing over for the past few weeks. I need to get this whole *I got married without telling anyone* conversation done while he's still here, to make sure Pops doesn't kill me.

I told Theo about the *Vegas* situation, which he seemed to dismiss as another hitch in my messed-up love life. Although I'm wondering if, after the five orgasms I gave her this afternoon, Savvy's finally coming around to the idea of staying married. Not that it matters if she's not, because I sure as shit am not divorcing her. No matter how much she asks for it. I have no doubt that (over time) she'll see things my way. She'll see that this, she and I, was always going to happen.

We're sitting around the dinner table. Everyone is here. Mom, Dad, Theo, Romeo, and Luca. Then there's my aunt and uncle—Pops likes to refer to them as the loose cannons of the family. Aunt Reilly is fiery as all hell, and my Uncle Bray was an undefeated cage fighter back in his day. Rumor has it that my uncle knocked my dad out one time and lived to tell the story. And I know for a fact my old man still holds a grudge about it.

Then there're my cousins Lily and Hope, also twins, who look like younger versions of my mom and Aunt Reilly. The newest additions are their husbands. Alex, who isn't as bad as I first thought. And Chase, who *is* just as bad as I first thought. I'm not really sure what Hope fucking sees in his pansy, rich-boy ass. He's the classic *rags to riches* story. I knew him before he got with my cousin though, and that's the problem. I know how much of a player he was—although even I can't deny how attached he seems to be. If he's not following my cousin around like a damn lost puppy, his eyes are.

Savvy is sitting next to me. My hand rests on her leg under the table, and for once, she hasn't pushed it off. "I, uh, I have some news," I announce to everyone.

The whole table quietens. Savvy tenses beside me, her head pivots in my direction, and her eyes widen. I search her face. If she really wants me to stop, I will. She knows what I'm about to say, and although I can feel the tremor in her leg under my open palm, she's not stopping me. I grab her hand and entwine my fingers with hers.

Looking directly into her eyes, and not those of my entire family, I clear my throat. "Savannah and I got married."

She gives me a small smile. Nobody says a word, and after a moment, I tear my eyes from Savannah and focus them on the rest of the occupants of the room. No one even looks surprised—well, no one except my dad. He has that unreadable, blank expression on his face. He's either going to shoot me or congratulate me. Though, judging by the way he's white-knuckling the steak knife in his hand, I'm assuming it's not going to be the latter.

"Ah, crap, I have that thing. You know that thing, Bray? I need your help," Aunt Reilly says, standing and pulling Uncle Bray along with her.

"Oh yeah, that's right. Girls, you too. Out now." He

nods towards his daughters. Before long, the room is cleared. The only ones left are my parents, Savannah and me, and my three brothers who are all looking at me with identical smiles on their faces. I think they're just glad to not be on the other end of our dad's wrath for once.

"I'm going to need you to repeat that, Matteo, because I swear you just said you and Savannah got married." Dad uses that tone I've heard him use on business associates—the sort who aren't left breathing when he's done with them.

Shit, he's more pissed than I thought he would be. I don't really give a shit though. Savannah is mine, and not even my old man will be taking that away from me. "I did say that. Exactly that." Savannah is so tense beside me I think she's going to pass out. I lean into her ear. "Breathe, babe. It's okay," I whisper and watch as her chest deflates to release the air she was holding back.

I wait for what seems like forever before Dad looks at Savvy. "Savannah, were you a willing party to these nuptials?" he asks her.

"What the fuck? Of course she was fucking willing," I answer for her.

"Pops, seriously, as if he'd force her to do anything," Theo grunts.

Ignoring my brother, Dad keeps his eyes on me. "Watch your mouth, Matteo. I was asking her, not you," he grinds out, pointing the tip of the knife at me. Mom eyes his grip before taking the knife from his hand and placing it on the other side of her plate—far out of his reach. I'm not a fool though. My father doesn't need a weapon when he still has his hands.

"Ah, it's okay. We were—well, we were drunk and in Vegas. But, yes, I was willing," Savannah says.

"You were drunk and in Vegas. Great, that's the story my grandchildren are going to fucking hear about their parents' wedding day." My dad curses under his breath. Then he directs a finger at us. "You'll have a proper wedding, a formal one. One your mother has been looking forward to since you were both fucking six years old. I will not allow you to take that away from her, Matteo."

"If it helps, I'll be getting hitched soon, Ma. You can plan my wedding." Theo smirks. I know he's trying to defuse the tension and I'm thankful for his efforts.

"Not the time, Theo, but we will discuss this further later on," Mom says before turning to Pops. "T, it's fine, really. Tell Savannah how grateful we are to have her formally join our family and let them be."

"Well, I, for one, *am* grateful. Who woulda thought we'd get such a hot sister-in-law?" Luca nudges Romeo in the shoulder.

My head snaps to both of them. "Call her hot again and I'll rip your fucking tongues out of your mouths," I warn them.

"Matteo, stop. You're not touching your brothers," Mom scolds me.

"Savannah, we are extremely grateful to have you join our family. Not that you weren't already a part of it," My dad says before adding, "Matteo, follow me." He pushes his chair back, stands, and walks out of the room.

Savvy's hand grips mine tighter, and her worried eyes bore into mine, pleading with me not to follow him. As ruthless as my father may be, he's not going to do any real damage to me. He's far too scared of my mother's wrath to even try it. Besides, I am his favorite son. He won't admit it, but I don't need him to. How could I not be the favorite?

"It's fine. I'll meet you upstairs in a bit. Don't worry," I whisper to Savvy before placing a soft kiss on the top of her head as I stand. I exit the room, and Theo follows me out. We make our way to the living room, where there's a wet bar, because I'm certain that's where I'm going to find him.

Sure enough, by the time we get there, a glass of whiskey is firmly gripped in each of my father's hands. I take the one offered to me, but don't bring it to my mouth just yet. I wait. I know my old man, and whatever he has to say, he'll get to it when he's ready. Sometimes I think he does these long, silent pauses on purpose, just to make the other person sweat. Me, I'm not the least bit worried.

Okay, maybe a little. But not a lot. I do want my family to accept the new relationship between Savvy and me, because this dynamic isn't changing.

"I don't know whether to congratulate you or slap some fucking sense into you, boy," Pops says, shaking his head as he sits on a single wingback chair.

"I'll take the congratulations." I smile, holding my glass in the air, then finally bring it to my lips. The smoothness of the whiskey runs down my throat like an old friend. A much-appreciated burn following its path. I do my best not to squirm under my father's piercing gaze.

"I can't say I'm not disappointed about how you went about this. Your mother has been looking forward to each of your weddings. Especially yours."

"Why mine?" I ask. She still has three other sons, all painfully single.

"Because we always knew it'd be with Savannah. That's why," he says. "Tell me why she's had a sudden change of heart. I know she's had her... *reservations* when it comes to what we do. What you do. So how is that going to change?"

I feel like my plan of keeping her so high on orgasmic bliss that she doesn't have the capacity to think of anything else won't go over well with my father. So I go for honesty. "She's not exactly on board with it. But she's getting there. She will get there," I say with determination.

Pops pauses his glass midair and his eyes scrunch up. "What do you mean she's not on board? I swear to God, Matteo, if you're forcing this girl into anything she doesn't want to do, it will not end well for you." His tone is harsh.

Theo stands between us. He's silent, but I know my brother's ready to jump in at any point if this gets too heated. Don't get me wrong, I'm thankful my family is protective of Savannah. But, fuck, I'm the last fucking person on earth who would ever hurt her. "I didn't fucking force her. Is it really that unfathomable that she actually loves me?" I avoid his first question while offering one of my own.

"No, I know she does. But answer the fucking question. How is she not on board?"

I sigh, running my free hand through my hair. "We were drunk. The next day, she asked me to draw up divorce papers."

"And you didn't?"

"I'm not fucking divorcing her," I grunt.

"Fucking hell. Matteo, you can't force her into a family like ours if she doesn't want to be a part of it."

"She does. She just needs a little time to get used to the idea. That's all."

"I hope, for your sake, you're right," Pops says. "For all of our sakes," he tacks on with a sigh.

"I can't let her go," I tell him. "I don't know how to."

"Sometimes we don't get a choice, son." He stands, setting the empty glass on the table beside him. "Don't fuck up. I like Savannah, more than I like you." He laughs before exiting the room. I don't take his words to heart. I know he cares for Savvy, but nothing is more important to him than blood.

"She will come around, Matteo. That girl loves you. There's never been any doubt about that. You just have to prove to her that you can give her the life she wants and still be who you are," Theo says with a palm firmly planted on my shoulder.

"Yeah, that should be easy." Sarcasm drips from my voice.

"You don't have a choice. If you can't do that, then you will lose her."

"I know."

"I gotta go. You gonna be all right here?" he asks.

"Yep, just fucking dandy." I go in search of my wife. I have a few more orgasms to hand out tonight, and I know she'll be worried about my conversation with Pops.

23

SAVVY

Listen to advice and accept discipline, and at the end you will be counted among the wise.

Proverbs 19:20

I've been hiding out in my bedroom all day. I can't bring myself to face everyone after Matteo's announcement over the dinner table last night. He's been in here most of the day with me. I'm more convinced now than ever that he's trying to kill me by orgasm. At this point, I think I've had more pleasure in the last week with Matteo than I've had in my entire adult life. I'm not complaining, but I do wonder whether he's making up for lost time or just trying to blind me to something, by keeping me in a state of blissful ignorance.

He told me his conversation with his dad last night went well. That his family is, of course, over the moon that we're married. I can't say when the news reaches my own father that he'll feel the same way. That is a conversation I'll be avoiding for as long as I can.

Stepping out of the bathroom, I tuck the corner of the towel into itself to hold it in place, and when I look up, I'm greeted by Matteo's heated gaze running along the length of me. "Fucking perfection, Savvy," he says, but there's something in his tone—a hesitance I'm not used to hearing.

"What's wrong?" I ask, frozen to the spot.

"Nothing's wrong. I... uh..." Matteo rubs a hand over the back of his neck. "I have to return to New York early. Something's come up."

I call bullshit. However, letting it go for now, I ask, "Okay, that's fine. When do we leave?"

"That's the thing... I'm going. Alone. I need you to stay here, with my parents. They're planning on flying home in a couple of days."

That is exactly what I didn't want. I know I've never asked much about his *work* before, but he's never flat-out hidden a lot from me either. I know there's something he's not telling me. Has our relationship always been like this? Is it me who's changing? Now that we're supposed to be married, am I the one asking questions I've never asked before?

"Okay, when you're in New York, get those papers ready, Matteo. Because this... it's never going to work when you're blatantly keeping shit from me."

"I'm not keeping shit from you, Savvy. There's just some stuff you don't need to worry about. Business stuff you're far better off not knowing."

I tilt my head at him. "Why are you going back to New York early, Matteo?"

"Theo fucked up. The twins and I are heading home to make sure he doesn't make an even bigger mess than he already has."

"What'd he do?"

"*That* I can't tell you, babe. You know I can't." His tone is pleading.

"I've told you before, Matteo... I can't sit around and wait. I'm gonna go crazy, wondering where you are, if your safe, if your heart is still beating. Don't do that to me."

"I don't know what else to do, Savvy. I need to make sure you're safe, and right now, the safest place for you is here with my parents."

I shake my head. "And what about you? Who's making sure you're safe, Matteo?"

He smirks at my question. "Babe, I have a whole army of soldiers around me. I'm going to be fine. I'll be crashing at Theo's penthouse until you return. Then I swear we're leaving for Melbourne. By New Year's, we'll be there."

"Matteo, where do you see us in five years? Ten?"

I'm struggling to envision how this marriage is going to work. Do I love him? More than anything, but I'm not prepared to sit back and watch him get killed either.

He stands and saunters towards me. "I see us... *together*. That's where I see us in five, ten, twenty, fifty years. As long as we're together, Savvy, we will leap over any hurdles that come our way. I believe we have the kind of love worth fighting for. I can't fight alone though. I need you right alongside me, fighting with me." He cups the back of my neck in one hand. Leaning in, he peppers featherlight kisses on my lips. "Can you do that? For us, for me. Can you promise me to fight whatever demons or doubts you're still having about us?"

When he's this close to me, it's hard to think straight. It's hard to remember what my argument even was to begin with. I nod my head. "I'll try."

"That's all I ask," he says before claiming my lips in a much more determined kiss. This kiss says everything. It's one of ownership.

His tongue slips inside my mouth. He tastes of whiskey and something else—something that's entirely unique to Matteo. I can't quite put my finger on the flavor. But, whatever it is, it's intoxicating. Addictive. My arms wrap around his neck, pulling him closer to me. My body shamelessly rubs up against his.

Matteo pulls away from my mouth, nibbling a trail along my jaw. "I need to fuck you, Savvy, and it's not going to be soft or gentle. I can't leave here without knowing the imprint of my cock will be lining the walls of your pussy for days." His voice is husky, full of need.

My whole core tightens at the thought of what he's just promised. "Are you sure you're up to the task? That's a tall order, Tao," I ask him, as my hand cups his already-hard cock through his slacks.

Matteo takes a step backwards. As he does, he pulls on my towel, making it drop to the floor. I'm standing here, completely naked. But I don't think it's just my exterior that's been bared to him right now. I feel like my whole soul is on display.

"Fuck me, I love your fucking body, Savvy. So goddamn perfect. Every fucking inch of it. And it's mine." He doesn't move as his eyes trail up from my toes to my head.

I do my best not to squirm, but it's hard fighting the urge to cover myself up. The fact that Matteo is still fully clothed in a dress shirt and pants, while I stand naked, is more arousing than I would have thought. There's something about being at his mercy that turns me on more than I want to admit.

"I want you on the bed. On your hands and knees. I want that ass of yours in the air for me, Savvy," he demands.

I can feel myself getting wetter by the minute. I'm so conflicted, torn between following his orders or telling him how things are going to be happening.

"Now! Don't make me ask again," he says in a more authoritative tone. And fuck, does my pussy gush at the sound.

My inner feminist is cursing me out right now, but I'm shutting her up. I want this. I want whatever Matteo is about to give me, because I know it's going to be damn good.

I climb onto the bed, on all fours, my wet hair hanging over my shoulder as I turn my head back to watch Matteo. He takes his time closing the distance between us. His right hand cups my bare ass. Squeezing. Massaging. Before he lifts his open palm and brings it down with a harsh slap. "Ow, fuck!" I catch myself before I fall forward on the mattress.

"That's for not doing what I asked the first time," he says, rubbing a hand over the raw imprint. It isn't long until the slight pain turns into pleasure building in my core. I don't have time to reflect on this sensation before I feel his lips kissing over that still-tender spot.

I tense when his mouth nears my puckered hole. Surely he's not going to...

"Oh shit," I cry out as his tongue licks around that forbidden area. This isn't something we've ever done. It's not something *I've* ever done—or ever had done to me.

"Every fucking inch of you is mine, Savvy. Mine to do with as I please. Mine to cherish," he says as he rubs my hole with a finger.

I can't help but squirm beneath his touch. It feels so

good, yet so wrong. His finger dips down to my wet pussy, pushing in and out a few times before he brings it back to my other hole. He slowly inches his finger inside, and my face falls to the mattress, the pillowtop muffling the moans that Matteo's touch elicits from me. "Oh god."

"You like that, don't you? Wait until it's my cock buried in this little hole of yours instead," he says, moving his finger in and out of my ass.

I find myself pushing back towards him, seeking more. More of him. More of anything. "Tao, please, I need..."

"I know what you need, babe. I got it right here for you."

I lift my head slightly, to peer over my shoulder, and see him stroking himself. My hips push backwards on their own. That's what I want. I want that in me. I can feel myself leaking down my thighs. I'm about to beg him to put it in, to fuck me like only he can, when I feel the tip of his cock at the entrance of my pussy.

Matteo removes his finger from my ass. One hand trails up my back, stopping at where my neck meets my hairline, and he grips tightly. Holding me in place. Not that I was planning on going anywhere. His other hand grabs my hip—a hip that already displays the bruising from everything we've done this past week. My body is covered in small black and blue fingerprints. Without warning, Matteo thrusts into me, literally taking the breath from my lungs.

"Fuck, your pussy is so goddamn good. I'll never get enough of this, Savvy," he says, pulling out only to thrust back in.

"Fuck, oh god, Matteo, harder," I urge him on. I don't want him holding anything back.

"As you wish." He responds by leaning his body forward, over the top of me, and he starts fucking me just like he promised. He fucks me so hard, fast, and rough that I have no doubt I'll be feeling his touch for days. "I want you to come for me, Savvy. Drench my cock with your juices. I want to feel you weeping all over me."

His hand moves from my neck to just under my hips, then his finger is pressing on my clit. Rubbing in circles. That's all it takes to have me soaring high. My body spasms as he fucks me through one orgasm right into the next. I can hear myself saying something—nothing coherent though.

"Fuck, I'm going to come. I'm going to paint your pussy with my cum, Savvy," Matteo grits out between thrusts as I feel him do just that. Warm liquid squirts inside me. We both collapse onto the mattress. Matteo rolls to his side as I lie flat on my stomach. I'm way too worn out to move a single muscle just yet. "Are you okay?" he asks, pulling my hair away from my face.

"Uh-huh." That's about the only kind of answer he's getting from me right now.

"I love you, Savannah. Never forget that." He kisses my forehead.

"I love you too," I tell him. Love isn't the issue between us. I'm the issue; my fear is the issue. "Are you sure you can't take me with you? What if I need you? A couple of days is a really long time without these magical orgasms you keep giving me." I smile.

"Magical, huh?" Matteo beams at the compliment. "Don't worry, babe, I'm sure I can make you come over the phone."

And I don't doubt that.

24

MATTEO

My eldest brother sees the spirit of sickness and removes it before it takes shape, so his name does not get out of the house. My elder brother cures sickness when it is still extremely minute, so his name does not get out of the neighborhood. As for me, I puncture veins, prescribe potions, and massage skin, so from time to time my name gets out and is heard among the lords.

— Sun Tzu, The Art of War

I've spent more time in the gym today than I ever have before. Thankfully, Theo is a vain-ass bastard and has a full setup in his penthouse. I have so much repressed energy—which I'd much rather be working out on top of Savvy. I'm pissed I had to leave her behind to come back to New York early. I can't really blame Theo though, because if I had walked in on Savvy in a similar situation to the one Maddie got herself into, it would have been a much bigger bloodbath.

Maddie thought she was starting a new waitressing job in a strip club. She didn't know that, that particular club auctioned their staff off to the highest bidder. When Theo heard she'd gone there, he'd made it just in time before anything happened to her. Although the two men who had their hands on her ended up with bullet holes for third eyes.

Usually it wouldn't have been a problem. Except those two men belonged to another crime family. We're not supposed to be at war with the other Italian branches. I've been waiting for the blowback, for the retaliation to come. It's why I made sure Savvy didn't return with me. Except there hasn't been anything.

Nothing. It's unusually quiet on the streets of New York City. Cold and fucking quiet. Theo is out meeting with Harry Gambino as we speak. I have the worst feeling in my gut—a feeling I can't shake. Something is gonna go wrong. I should have gone with him. I would have if he wasn't so insistent on me staying here to protect Maddie and her little sister, Lilah. I did make sure my brother had backup, not that he knows about it. My Uncle Neo, Aunt Angelica, and cousin Izzy are all there. On the street. Watching his sit-down.

I'm pacing the foyer area when Neo and Izzy drag in a disgruntled, bleeding-out Theo. A string of fast-flowing Italian is yelled to the room before my uncle tells Luca and me to take our big brother to the gym. We have to bypass the hurricane that is Maddie, who looks like she's ready to murder all of us. We lay him down on the makeshift hospital bed, seconds before the little spitfire storms in behind us, demanding answers.

I smirk when Theo notices her state of dress. "Maddie, where are your fucking clothes?" he growls. "Go put some on."

"Make me!" she demands with her arms folded over her chest. My brother attempts to sit upright, likely looking to call her bluff.

"Don't move." The doctor pushes him back down on the bed. "Boys, help me turn him." I lift Theo's shoulder, supporting his weight while Doc inspects his back. "It's a clean through and through," the doctor says after a beat, and I sigh in relief. This isn't the first time and probably won't be the last time I have to watch one of my brothers getting stitched up after a gunfight.

Once Theo is pieced back together, I head into the guest room and straight for the shower. A few more days and I'll have Savvy in my arms again. Sitting on the bed in a pair of sweats, I send her a text.

ME:

Wifey, what are you wearing?

I see the read indication pop up immediately and then the three little dots that tell me she's writing a reply.

MY WIFE:

> Wifey? Really, Tao. No, just no.

I smile at her reply—*don't think she's a fan of the new nickname.* The dots appear again, followed by another message from her.

MY WIFE:

> I'm wearing a black thong, no bra, and one of your white t-shirts.

Fuck, that image she just put in my head makes my dick hard. I make a point to tell her as much.

Me:

My cock just got hard.

My wife:

> Well, if you had taken me with you, maybe you'd have a way to work out that hard-cock situation of yours.

Fuck me, she's torturing me. I start writing a reply when I hit the green phone button and call her instead. She takes her time. I almost expect it to ring out when she finally answers. "Hello." The sound of her breathy voice coming through calms my nerves.

"Hey, babe, miss me?"

"Mmm, a little bit. What are you doing?" she asks.

"I'm sitting here with my cock in my hand, wishing it was buried deep inside your pussy." I slip an open palm under the waistband of my sweats and wrap it around my cock.

"Ah, okay," she says on a hitched breath. "Hey, remember that time we were nine and I dared you to lick the frozen flagpole and your tongue got stuck like that kid in that movie?"

"Unfortunately," I tell her. "Savvy?"

"Yeah?"

"Stop stalling. I want your fingers rubbing on that pretty little clit of yours. Now."

"Ah, yep, sorry. That thought will have to wait for another time." She laughs.

"This isn't a laughing matter, Savvy. My cock is hard, weeping. He fucking misses you."

"Your mom says hi."

And with those words, my boner is deflating. "What the fuck, Savvy?"

"Uh-huh, I will... She's right here. Want me to put her on?" she asks.

"No, if I wanted to talk to my mother, I would have called her. I called you. You and that delicious pussy of yours. That's who I want to speak to. You know what? Just hold the phone out to your cunt. Let me talk to it."

"Um, no. I gotta go. I'm playing chess with your mom, and she's waiting for me."

"She can wait. I need you."

"I'll call you back later."

"I love you."

"I love you too." The phone clicks off, and I'm left pouting over the fact my mother is getting to spend time with Savvy when it should be my turn.

It's New Year's Day and I'm on fucking edge, waiting for Savvy to land back in the city. It was easier spending days apart before I had the taste of her on my tongue. Before I knew I could sink my cock into her whenever I wanted, however I wanted.

Don't get me wrong: it's not just her pussy that I miss. I miss the whole fucking package. Savannah has always been—and will always be—the best thing I've ever had in my life. The day we became friends, back when we were six years old, was one of my smarter life decisions.

I'm getting dressed, preparing to meet her at the private hanger, when I get a message.

My wife: Just landed. Rocco is driving me back to your place now.

Me: Our place. And I'll meet you there.

My wife: I think your dad wants to see you first. He was really antsy on the flight, more so than usual.

Before I can respond, I get a message from the man himself.

Boss: Don't leave Theo's place until I get there. I need to talk to all of you.

I send him a quick reply.

Me: Make it fast. I've got things to do, people to see, Pops.

He doesn't answer. I didn't expect him to. Instead, I open the chat with Savvy again.

Me: I'll be there as soon as I can. Wait for me in bed. Naked.

She sends back a red heart emoji and a wink face.

"Matteo! Get your ass out here now!" Theo's pissed-off voice rings out through the penthouse. Rolling my eyes, I walk out towards the main living room. "Who the fuck made her cry?" he booms at the twins while gesturing towards Lilah.

She's only sixteen and been under Maddie's legal guardianship since both their parents died two years ago. Theo has taken on somewhat of a caregiver role to the girl, more so when he found out she was on the transplant list and in dire need of a new kidney—*so God help anyone who upsets or tries to touch the kid.*

"What's going on?" I ask.

"Where were you while these two fucking heathens were destroying my fucking living room?" Theo snarls at me before pivoting back to our baby brothers. "And I'm still waiting for an answer from *you*?" His voice echoes off the walls.

"Uh, Theo, I'm fine. Really, it wasn't them," Lilah says in their defense.

"Then why are you crying?" he asks her.

"Um, I may have overheard Luca tell Romeo about the kidney thing... that he's going to give me a kidney," she says in the quietest voice.

Well, that's fucking news to me too.

Theo points at the twins. "My office, now!" Then he shoves Romeo towards the hall that leads to the office, and Luca's not far behind him. I trail after them to make sure my older brother doesn't actually kill the bastards.

I expected Theo to keep following but he stays in the living room. Once I'm in the office, I help myself to my brother's top-shelf whiskey. "So what are you two idiots fighting over anyway?" I ask the twins.

"Nothing," they both answer at the same time.

"Riiiight, so Theo's living room looks like a hurricane has blown through it over *nothing*? That's what I'm supposed to believe?"

They shoot a glance at each other, as tight-lipped as a pair of priests at a peepshow. They've always been this way—not even I can torture the words out of them if I tried. They have that weird twin-bond thing going on. I down the whiskey right as the door to the office opens, and my dad walks in, followed by Theo.

"Pops, I didn't know you were coming in today," Luca says.

"Clearly," Dad replies. After pouring himself a

drink, he turns to the twins. "Care to explain why your brother's home looks like a hurricane ran through it?"

That's what I said.

I smirk but don't voice the thoughts in my head, while the boys share a look—that same oddly cryptic look. "We just had a minor disagreement. It's nothing. Water under the bridge," Romeo grinds his teeth.

"You're brothers. You're on the same fucking team. We have enough people trying to kill us without killing each other. Whatever *this* is, sort it out. And whatever Theo has to replace out there." Dad gestures to the door. "...it's coming out of your allowances."

I laugh. Not even I would want to replace Theo's expensive-ass shit.

"What? Pops, that's not fair," Luca argues.

"What's not fair is that your brother took a beating and a fucking bullet for your asses and then you come here and destroy his home."

The twins glance at Theo and their faces pale—which says a lot, considering how tan they are.

"What are you talking about? What do they have to do with the Russians who jumped me?" Theo asks.

"That's what I'm here to find out," Pops says, lowering himself down on one of the sofas. "Start talking,"

"Fuck," I say under my breath, then pour myself another whiskey before moving to stand next to Theo. I'm going to fucking strangle these little shits if they're the reason he was left to bleed out on the New York City sidewalk.

"It wasn't our fault," Luca says.

"It never fucking is," Theo grunts.

"He fucking deserved it. He hurt her in the worst way, so we put him in the hospital," Romeo adds.

"Who did you put in the hospital and who did they hurt?" Dad asks, and right now I'm fucking glad it's not me on the other end of his death stare.

"Livvy... That fucker attacked her. He...." Romeo trails off.

Fuck, this is all because of some girl?

"He hurt her, so we hurt him. Stephan Petrov. He deserved it, Pops, swear it," Luca says.

"Who is this Livvy?" Pops narrows his eyes on Romeo, ignoring Luca.

"She's, ah, my tutor."

Why the fuck does Romeo need a tutor? The kid's a goddamn genius.

"Romeo, you're trying my last nerve here, son. You have a fucking 4.0 GPA. Why the fuck do you need a tutor?" Dad asks the question that's running through my mind.

"I... I'm not sure. But she is, and I wasn't going to stand by and let that fucker get away with hurting her," Romeo hisses.

"Right," Dad says.

"It's fine, Pops. What's the plan from here?" Theo interjects, surprising the hell out of all of us.

"It's done. Eye for an eye and all that bullshit. We hospitalized one of theirs; they put a bullet through one of ours." Dad shrugs. "The Petrovs know nothing about those girls. And we need to fucking keep it that way." He throws an arm out towards the living room, gesturing to Maddie and Lilah, who we've recently discovered have both Italian *and* Russian mob ties.

Their mother was related to the Gambinos—a family we're on very friendly terms with. While their father was a Petrov—a family we most certainly are *not* on friendly terms with. All of us came to an agreement that we need to keep Maddie and Lilah's paternity under lock and key. We need to protect them from the potential repercussions that come with that knowledge. There was a reason their parents were on the run before their deaths, hiding in plain sight while living under pseudonyms. We just haven't figured it all out yet.

25

SAVVY

I am my beloved's and my beloved is mine.

Song of Solomon 6:3

The last few days without Matteo have given me time to think. Time away from being drunk on orgasms. And I've come up with two conclusions.

One, I undoubtedly—wholeheartedly—love Matteo Valentino and that scares the crap out of me. Two, I cannot walk away from him.

The days spent with his parents, without the boys around, have been eye-opening. The love that Mr. and Mrs. Valentino have for one another is so strong and fierce. I've always observed them together, watched how sincerely they care for each other, but not as much as I have over these last few days.

Their relationship is solid, and it's something I want for myself. It's something I already have with Matteo. I know the bond we share is unbreakable, despite my own fears trying to get between us. I'm thankful to Matteo that he hasn't given up on us. He knows what we have isn't something we'll ever find with anyone else. It goes beyond physical attraction; I do believe God put Matteo in my life for a reason. If we weren't meant to be, then this love wouldn't feel so all-consuming. It's almost like there is no me without Matteo; there is no Matteo without me. Which I know sounds like an extremely unhealthy attachment.

It's an attachment I'm not going to break though. I've decided that I'm not going to let the fear of tomorrow get in the way of our happiness. I just have to find a way to deal with it better. I may have gotten myself a little wasted on vodka, the first night Matteo left me behind in Canada. It did nothing to numb the anxiety that was crawling through my veins.

Rocco is driving me back to Matteo's house—no matter how much he insists that it's *ours*, it doesn't feel like that yet. I should probably start ordering furnishings and décor. Maybe then it will start feeling more like a home.

When we pull up to the gate, Rocco enters the code into the pin pad. It doesn't escape me that Matteo set the code as the date we first slept together when we were fifteen: Zero, four, thirteen. Rocco brings the vehicle to a stop in front of the house.

"Ma'am, I need you to wait here. I'll be back to get you." He jumps out of the car, locking the doors behind him with the remote as he jogs up the steps to the front door.

I figure it's some stupid new routine check that Matteo's making him do before I go inside the house. I pull out my phone and send an email to Kirstin. There is a lot that needs to be organized before I can jet-set across the world with Matteo. I have to finalize the purchases and coordinate the deliveries for Loch Neilson's penthouse. I'm going to have to put Kirstin on the staging of that one. I won't have time to fit it in. I know she can manage this on her own. I've trained her myself, to be just as pedantic about the finer details as I am.

I press send on my to-do list to my assistant and drop my phone back into my bag. I look up to see two bright lights through the window of the bottom level of the house. These are accompanied by the unmistakable sound of gunshots.

Shit, shit. What do I do?

I consider jumping over the seat and driving away, but Rocco took the keys with him. Pulling at the door handle only confirms that the car is locked. I duck down, out of the windows' view, and hit call on Loch Neilson's phone number. He's the only one I know that can unlock this car from a computer.

"Mrs. Valentino, this is a surprise," he answers.

"I need you to unlock the car again," I whisper,

though I don't know why. It just seems like I should keep my voice down.

"I can't do that. Your husband will kill me," he argues.

"Please, Loch, I'm stuck in this locked car and there're gunshots going off inside the house. I need to get out of here. Please," I beg him.

"Fuck, shit, okay. Hold on. Give me two minutes." Loch curses under his breath, the sound of him tapping furiously on a keyboard in the background.

"I don't have two minutes. I need to get out of here."

"Okay, I'm working as fast as I can, Savannah. Your husband's had some kind of extra security layers added to the car's software."

"Shit, can you get past them?" I ask him. My hand reaches under the seats. Surely there's a weapon in here somewhere.

He laughs in reply. "Is the Pope Catholic?"

"Loch, if something happens, if I don't... tell Matteo that I love him and I don't want the papers anymore."

"Stop, you're going to be fine. Keep your phone on you," Loch says. "The doors should open now."

I search under the other seat and my palm wraps around something cold and metal. I send up a prayer of thanks as I retrieve a handgun. I check that it's loaded and thank God again. Pulling on the handle, I push the car door open. "It worked. Thank you, Loch. Thank you," I whisper as I climb out.

"Savannah, stay on the phone. I want you to find

somewhere to hide, until your husband gets there. He's on his way."

"He is?"

"Yes, he is. I've been messaging him. Just be careful."

I sigh in relief at the thought, but then the fear that Matteo's going to end up hurt settles in. I don't know what to do. I make it to the side of the house. There's a line of trees that boarders the property. I'm about to make a run for it when a man appears from around the corner. He stares at me a minute before he starts walking towards me.

Without thinking, I raise the gun in my hand and pull the trigger. I see him stop, fall, and then I run. Heading straight for the woods. I can hear yelling behind me. I don't look back. I just keep running. Passing the clearing, I reach the tree line and take a moment to peer over my shoulder. I can't see much, but my instincts tell me to move. So I keep running. My legs burn; my lungs struggle for breath. I don't hear anything behind me but I can't stop.

There's so much vegetation, so many low-hanging branches that I struggle to push my way through. I jump over a fallen trunk and my foot lands at an odd angle. I hear the audible snap as I fall to the ground. My hand comes up to muffle my scream of agony.

"Fuck, fuck, shit," I curse as I use whatever strength I have left to sit upright. A searing pain rips through my ankle and it's already visibly swollen. I'm not a doctor, but judging by the look of it, I'm certain it's broken.

Shuffling along the ground, I rest my back against the trunk of a tree, hugging the handgun to my chest. This is it. They're going to find me. I can't run anymore. I can't do anything but sit here and wait.

I must have dropped my phone when I ran. I can't even recall when or where it likely landed. Leaning my head against the tree, I look up through the branches to the sky. "Please, God, I know it's been a while since I've been to church, but please let Matteo be okay. Let him find an even bigger love than me. Let him find peace."

I have so many regrets. I've wasted so much of our time together allowing my fears to hold me back. Silent tears stream down my cheeks. I don't want this to be the end. I want the life Matteo has always envisioned for us.

My ears strain to listen in the distance as I wait for them to find me. Whoever they are. I really hope it wasn't Rocco on the other end of those shots I heard. I was starting to grow attached to his grumpy ass. Plus, I know how much Matteo likes and trusts him.

I don't know how long I've been sitting against this tree. But the sky is darkening and it's cold. So cold. My body shivers. I pull my coat around me tighter while reaching for leaves, branches, anything I can use to cover myself to try to stay warmer. Everything I touch is damp and cold. There's no use.

Matteo... My mind drifts to him. Where is he? Has

he already made it to the house? I can't hear anything other than the sounds of birds chirping in the branches, the scurrying of what have to be animals. I need to try to get out of these woods, maybe crawl back towards the house. I couldn't have gotten that far.

Even as I think of moving, I can't force my limbs to comply. He'll find me. He always does. I'm doing my best to keep my eyes open, to not fall asleep. I can't protect myself if I fall asleep. It's hard though. My lids are getting heavier and heavier. I keep waking with a start every time I drift off for a brief moment.

26

MATTEO

There are five ways of attacking with fire. The first is to burn soldiers in their camp; the second is to burn stores; the third is to burn baggage trains; the fourth is to burn arsenals and magazines; the fifth is to hurl dropping fire amongst the enemy.

— Sun Tzu, The Art of War

*N*ew York has seen its fair share of mafia wars between rival families. But nothing can prepare the city for the hell I intend on raining down on it. I won't just burn this whole place to the ground. I'll maim, kill, torture anyone—anything that tries to get in my way.

Whoever the fuck thought they could take her from

me will rue the day they were born. I won't stop at the fuckers involved firsthand. No, I'll hunt down every last living member of their whole goddamn bloodline.

I'm staring at the dead fucker sprawled out across the lawn at the side of the house. My house, my and Savvy's house. A house that's supposed to be a safe place for her. I promised her that I'd never let anyone hurt her, never let anything happen to her, and I failed.

I fucked up.

I kick at his body. There's blood pooled around him. I want to bring him back to life, just so I can kill him slowly myself. What the fuck happened out here? I walked inside to find Rocco on the floor of an empty living room, a bullet between his eyes.

"Boss," Christian calls out to me.

I turn around and glare at him. I don't know why the fuck he's here. He mustn't have any sense of self-preservation, because right now I'm liable to strangle anyone in my line of sight.

"This hers?" he asks, holding up a phone.

I snatch it out of his hands. It's Savvy's. I type in her password and hit the last number in her call log. Fucking Loch Neilson. I swear that fucker is every-where he shouldn't be.

"Savannah?" he answers.

"No, it's her husband. Where the fuck is my wife?" I growl through the receiver.

"I-I don't know. I was talking to her and then the line cut out."

"When? How long ago was that?" I ask him.

"Ten minutes or so. I thought you must have gotten to the house," he adds quickly.

"You thought fucking wrong." I hang up.

"Ten minutes. She was on this phone ten minutes ago. They couldn't have gotten far. Fucking find them!" I yell. At this point, I'm not sure who I'm yelling at. Myself or my men.

"We're going to find her, Matteo," Christian says before pivoting on his heel, his gun drawn at the line of vehicles currently speeding along the driveway, closing in on my property.

He lowers his weapon. They're our cars. My brothers'. My father's. They jump out and run up to meet us. "Fuck. What the fuck happened here?" This comes from Theo.

I can't look at any of them. It's taking everything I have not to fall to the ground. I can't crumble though. Savvy needs me now more than ever. I have to find her. And when I do, when I know she's okay, I have to figure out a way to let her go, so nothing like this can ever happen to her again.

"She's gone." Two words that shatter my fucking soul—it's all I can say. All I can offer them. My brothers stare at me, waiting to stop the explosion I'm sure they're expecting.

My father's the one who steps up to me. He wraps his arms around my shoulders. "I swear we will fucking find her, Matteo. Don't let yourself think otherwise."

I nod my head. I can't find the words to reply. My body is vibrating with the need to hunt. The need to inflict pain. "Ten minutes, I was fucking ten minutes too late," I say, stepping back from my father's embrace.

"We'll find her," Theo says assuredly while tapping away at his phone.

"They couldn't have gotten far." *Yeah, that's what I was thinking.* But it doesn't bring comfort. "I'll have Zed track the traffic cams for anyone leaving this street over the last few minutes."

Zed is our usual go-to tech guru. He's good. But I know someone even better. "I've got another guy," I say, redialing Loch Neilson's number as I walk into the house. I might not have furniture in here, but I do have my very own arsenal in the basement.

"Did you find her?" he answers.

"I need you to hack into the city traffic cams. I'm sending you an address. I want details of every car that drove on this street in the last fifteen minutes. I want their license plates, the addresses of where they went," I say, ignoring his question. I can hear him typing. "Can you do it?" I ask.

He scoffs. "I'm already in. Send me the address."

"Just look for Hudson Street, Haleville," I tell him.

"Got it."

"Call me back when you have the details." I hang up, make my way down the stairs, and open the locked door to the safe room. I didn't even get a chance to show Savvy that the house had safe rooms.

Would she have made it in here if I had mentioned them?

I pick up a bag and open it. I then take an automatic rifle from the wall mount and place it inside, followed by another. And another. I walk around the room, picking up a range of guns, a few grenades, smoke bombs, and tear gas.

"Matteo, we need a plan. You don't even know where she is. What are you going to do? Shoot up the whole city?" Theo asks.

"If that's what it takes." I grab a separate bag and fill it with ammo.

"Bro, we've got your back. You know that. But be reasonable. You can't go in half-cocked on adrenaline with no plan of attack," Romeo adds.

I spin on him. *"Be reasonable?* My fucking wife has been taken," I yell. "My wife! And you expect me to be fucking reasonable? If you're not coming with me, then get the fuck out of my way." I hand the bags to Christian, who's been quietly observing us at a distance. At least he's not sharing his thoughts. "Let's go." I walk past my brothers.

My father must be upstairs still; he didn't follow us. As my foot hits the last step and I pivot, I note that sure enough he's in the foyer, yelling into his phone in rapid Italian. He sees me and hangs up. "What's the plan?" he asks at the same time Savvy's phone rings in my hand. I look at the screen. It's Loch.

"What have you got?" I ask him.

"Two cars, SUVs, left in a hurry. Eight minutes ago. They're still en route somewhere. I'm following their GPS signal. Both vehicles are registered to a guy named Victor Petrov."

I knew it was the fucking Russians—the bastards never fucking give up. First they sent in that Irish fucker to steal our shipments, then they attacked Theo, my men at the storefront, and now my home. My wife. Let's see how quickly they surrender when I storm their goddamn businesses. Their homes. Victimize their families.

"Send me the GPS coordinates." I hang up the phone and pass it to Christian. "Follow the tracking that's being sent through," I tell him. "It's the fucking Petrovs." My jaw grinds as rage floods my body, quickly followed by dread. If the Russians have Savvy, there's no telling what's happening to her. What they'll do to her. I need to fucking get to my wife before any of them have the chance to lay a finger on her. "Fuck!" I roar as my fist flies through the closest wall.

"Let's go," Pops says.

When I step outside, I find twenty cars waiting. All filled with our men. I didn't call them. I look to my father, giving him a nod. My gratitude.

I jump into the passenger seat. Christian is at the wheel. Just as I'm about to close myself inside the vehicle, the back doors open. Swinging around, I see all three of my brothers climbing in. I don't question why they're riding in my car and not their own. I know they're here because they think they can stop me from doing something stupid. Turning back to Christian, I take the phone off him. "Break every fucking road rule you have to. Just catch up to these fuckers."

His answer is nothing more than a smile and a nod, then tires are screeching out of the driveway. Nerves and thoughts I don't want to be dwelling on are consuming me.

Please just let her be okay. I know I've been a shitty fucking Catholic. But please, God, let her be okay. If you have to take a soul, take mine.

"Well, this takes the whole *drive it like you stole it* to a new level," Luca says from the back seat. Theo reaches over and slaps the kid upside the head. He doesn't say anything but I can imagine the glare he's sending Luca's way. It's one I've seen grown men piss themselves over.

"Left, take the next left. There're five minutes between us," I tell Christian.

"Got it," he says.

My fist opens and closes. I'm itching to get my hands on these fuckers. They're not going to know what hit them.

"Matteo, you know we're with you. Whatever you need us to do, just say the word," Theo says.

"What I need is my fucking wife back. I can't lose her," I tell him.

"You won't," he assures me.

"Two minutes," I tell Christian. He's closing in on them.

Theo's phone rings and I listen as he puts it on speaker. "We're going to surround the cars. Don't hit them. If Savannah is in one of those SUVs, we don't want her involved in a collision."

"Okay," we all agree with him.

"We've got three cars circling the perimeter. They'll block the road, and we'll come in behind them. Remember, unless you've got a clear shot and Savannah isn't in it, don't fucking chance it," Pops says.

When we pull in behind the two SUVs, I don't wait for the car to stop before I jump out. "Fuck, Matteo, wait the fuck up!" Theo yells. I hear the doors opening, the footsteps right behind me. I don't look back.

Whoever is occupying these cars, they're cowards and not getting out. Really, they're nothing more than sitting ducks right now. I walk up to the first SUV. The windows are blacked-out. I can't see shit. Christian and Romeo fall into step beside me. I look over to see Theo and Luca on the opposite side of the vehicle. Pops and a few of our other soldiers approach the second car, while at least twenty of our men surround the area, weapons drawn and aimed.

I glance at Theo again, and at my nod, we rip open the back doors. I don't ask questions or consider who's in the driver's seat before I'm pulling the trigger and putting a bullet in the back of the fucker's head. Theo follows suit. My eyes scan the interior. It's empty. No one else is here. She's not here. Spinning around, I approach the second car.

Pops has the driver ripped out of his seat and is holding him against the hood by his throat. "Where the fuck is she?" he asks. The fucker's turning blue from the lack of oxygen. Pops gives him a little shake before releasing some of the pressure around the guy's neck. I walked past them to peer inside the SUV.

She's not here either. Turning back, I look to my brothers. They're standing around with pity on their faces. I don't need their fucking pity at the moment.

"Where the fuck is she?" I ask no one in particular. I storm to our car and jump behind the wheel. But before I can get away from here, away from everyone, Theo slides into the passenger seat. He doesn't say anything as I shift into gear and drive off. It doesn't take long until I have two cars tailing me.

Fuck them. Fuck everyone.

27

SAVVY

So now faith, hope, and love abide, these three; but the greatest of these is love.

1 Corinthians 13:13

The sun streams through the openings in the trees above me. It's morning. I must have fallen asleep. I'm so cold. I know I need to move. I know if I stay here, I might as well give up now. I can't do that to Matteo.

Where is he? If he's looking for me, he must be going out of his mind. I need to get out of these woods. Attempting to pull myself to my feet—at least my knees

—I fall straight back down as searing pain radiates up my leg.

"Ahhhh." I scream out loud, not really caring who hears me now. The pain is almost unbearable. I can't just sit here and wait to be rescued though. If I do that, I'm not going to make it out of here.

Not alive anyway.

Tucking the pistol into the pocket of my jacket, I search for a branch I can use as a makeshift walking stick. I can't put any weight on my foot. I'm going to have to hop my way out of here. Why the hell did I think running into the woods was a good idea anyway? You'd think I'd never seen a horror movie. Everyone knows you don't run upstairs or into the dark woods. I'm surprised I still have a heartbeat at this point.

I shuffle on my hands and knees towards a branch that might work. Slowly rising while putting my weight on the broken tree limb, I get halfway up before the wood snaps and tiny pieces splinter into my hand. "Fuck!" I cry out and fall to my side, my palms taking the brunt of the impact.

I need to find a thicker branch. Something that won't crack under my weight. Either that, or crawl my way through these woods. When I get out of here, I'm making Matteo sell this damn house and buy something in the city. What was he thinking, moving us so far out of civilization? I know I'm exaggerating. This is a really nice neighborhood. Reserved for the one-percenters who can actually afford to live out here. But fuck, if he'd just picked something in the city, I wouldn't be in this predicament.

Five minutes later, my hands are scratched up and bleeding. I'm thankful I'm wearing jeans. I'd hate to see the state of my knees if I weren't. At least the denim is giving some sort of protection, even if it's just a little bit. My stomach growls. I'm hungry, thirsty, sore, and tired. All I want to do is lie down, go to sleep, and wake up in bed with Matteo—realizing this was all just a bad dream. I push through, ignoring my stomach while doing my best to block out the pain. Although that's nearly impossible. I ache everywhere. I'm not giving up. I will find my way back. I can't be that far into the woods. I'm trying to recall how long I was running, but I can't for the life of me remember.

"Thank you, God!" I look upwards, eyeing the long thick branch before taking it in my hands. This one feels stronger than the last one.

As carefully as I can manage, I rise to my knees, slowly transferring my weight onto the tree limb, and push to my one foot. My head spins as I stand upright. I reach out an arm to steady myself on the closest trunk.

"You can do this, Savvy. You have to," I tell my subconscious. Holding the branch in front of me, I hop on my good foot while hovering the other one above the ground. Pain shoots through my ankle as the blood rushes downward and it throbs with the beat of my heart. "Fuck, ow, fuck," I cry out.

Tears stream along my cheeks as a sense of hope-lessness washes over me. I'm stuck in the middle of the woods, it's freezing cold, and I'm probably going to die out here. And Matteo is going to find my lifeless body...

No. I can't do that to him. I have to get out of here. I will get out of here, even if it takes me all day.

🐾

IT'S BEEN HOURS. I don't even know how long I've been making my way through these woods. It's getting colder again. My energy level is almost depleted. My mouth is dry. How on earth did Jesus make it forty days in the desert? I can't even make it one day in the woods.

Stopping, I brace myself against a tree. I don't even know if I'm going the right way, or making my situation worse by going farther into the woods. I think I need to rest for a bit, and then I'll keep moving. I just need to close my eyes for five minutes, regroup, and somehow find the energy I need to keep pushing forward. Just five minutes.

I'm not sure how long I dozed off for. But when a pair of strong arms wrap around me, lifting me up, I snuggle into the warmth of the body. "I knew you'd find me, Tao," I mumble before fully giving in and allowing the darkness to take over.

28

MATTEO

In difficult ground, press on; in encircled ground, devise stratagems; in death ground, fight.

— Sun Tzu, The Art of War

It's been over twenty-four hours. She's gone. I don't know where the fuck she is and it's my fucking fault. How the hell am I supposed to find her when I have no idea who has her. The Russians seem to be as clueless as we are. That much is clear. We've had one of them chained up in the basement, and he's not saying shit. The dumb fucks screwed themselves, all because of a little spilled blood at a furniture store. They should know better than to try to attack us on the home front. But that's a problem for another day.

All that matters right now is my wife. Finding her and getting her back.

I pour myself some whiskey and bring it to my mouth, only to hurl the glass at the wall at the last minute. I don't deserve a goddamn drink.

Savvy is out there somewhere, probably scared, hurt, and enduring the worst possible treatment I can think of. Women do not fare well in this world of ours, not when they're weaponized. Whoever the fuck has her knows that she's my weakness. I will give up everything for her. Why the fuck hadn't I done it sooner? She begged me when we were teenagers, not to join the family, not to take the oath.

I should have fucking listened to her.

Falling to the ground, I let my head hang over my knees. I don't get to shed a tear. I don't deserve to wallow in the turmoil I'm feeling at not having her, not knowing where she is. It's my job to find her, and right now, I don't have the faintest clue as to what to do next. We've searched everywhere. Every nook and cranny of this goddamn house. The grounds and outer buildings. I look up and stare out the window. It's starting to get dark again. She's going to spend another night in hell.

"I'm going to need something of hers, Matteo. I've

got a guy bringing the dogs out here. We need a scent they can follow." Theo squats in front of me.

My gaze moves from the window to his face. "I need to find her, Theo. I can't... I don't know how... I need her," I plead with him.

"We are going to do everything we can to find her, Matteo. Don't give up just yet. Savannah is strong—remember that. She'll be fighting to get back to you." He puts a hand on my shoulder and squeezes.

"I don't think anyone is that strong, Theo. Look at what happened to Hope, how much it changed her," I remind him. Our cousin has never been the same after being date raped by her so-called boyfriend at sixteen. I know Savvy is strong, but no one is *that* strong.

"You don't know that's happening to Savannah. Let's not make shit up in our heads, and work with facts instead," Theo says, pushing to his feet to tower over me.

"Facts? The fact is my fucking wife is gone. Where the fuck is she? The fact is I was supposed to protect her from this sort of shit. And the fact is I fucking failed," I yell at him, rising to meet him chest to chest.

"You're right, and when we find her, you're going to do everything you have to do to fucking make it up to her. You're going to take her away, go on that fucking trip to Australia you were dead set on taking. Now, I need something with her scent on it."

I walk past him and head upstairs to the bedroom. I rip the pillowcase off the pillow she slept on. Bringing it to my nose, I inhale. It's all vanilla and cinnamon, all Savvy. Then I find a shirt she wore that's still sitting in the hamper before bringing the items back downstairs and handing them to Theo.

"Come on, they're waiting," he says, leading the way to the front of the house. "Jaxon." Theo nods to the scruffy-looking blonde guy with a dog.

"Theo, good to see you. Wish it were under better circumstances though," he offers in reply.

"This is my brother—Matteo." Theo introduces me to the man. He doesn't say anything, just gives a nod, which I'm thankful for. I'm not in the mood for small talk.

"You got the scent?" Jaxon asks.

"Yeah, here." Theo passes him the pillowcase and shirt.

"Where was the last known location?" This comes from a guy standing to the left of Jaxon with another dog.

"Around the side of the house," I tell them.

"Okay, it's best to start there. Lead the way," Jaxon says.

When we get around to the other side of the house, my stomach sinks. This is the last place she stood—as far as we'd determined.

Where did you go, Savvy?

I watch as Jaxon hands the shirt over to his counterpart, whose name I never got, not that I care who the fuck he is right now. If these dogs can find Savvy, I'll be eternally indebted to them. As soon as the dogs get a whiff of the fabric, they both start charging towards the woods. No, that can't be where she is. Those woods are dense, wet, and fucking cold. There's only one reason a man in our line of work would take someone to a place like that.

To dig a shallow grave. To bury something they don't want found.

I follow after the men and their dogs. They're sniffing wildly, not stopping. Not slowing down. My heart hammers in my chest the closer we get to the clearing before the grounds turn into straight-up woodlands. And sure enough, the dogs keep going, disappearing into the tree line.

The sun's going down. It's going to be dark soon. "Theo, get all the men, flashlights, whatever fucking lights the fuck up. I want this whole goddamn area searched," I tell him.

He nods and runs back towards the house. As my feet pound the soft earth, I try not to think of the worst, not picture her lifeless body buried in a fresh grave. It's fucking hard though. I guess that's what I get for having buried one too many bodies myself. Is this my karma? God's way of laughing at me? Teaching me a lesson? Giving me what I've always wanted, only to take it away? To make me suffer the most agonizing pain imaginable?

I make a vow to follow her. If she's left this world, then I'm not far behind. Because there is nothing here for me without her. I'd like to think I'd feel it, feel as though I were being cut in two, as half of my own soul —the good half—went up to heaven. While the rest of me is left to rot. Because, let's face it, Savvy's the only good part of me there is.

I have to believe she's still alive, because I don't feel... *that*. I feel a lot of things right now, but that isn't one of them. "How accurate are these dogs?" I ask Jaxon.

"Very. She definitely went this way," he says. Ten minutes later, the dogs stop by a tree. I look down and see tiny droplets of blood on the trunk.

"Fuck," I curse under my breath. I touch the blood. It's dried up. Not that fresh. Is it hers? With the way the dogs are sniffing at it wildly, I'm betting it is.

"You might want to call in every resource you have at your disposal. It's getting dark and she's out here, hurt..." He lets his words trail off.

I don't need him to finish them. I know how dire the situation is. It's so cold. Could she have even survived the first night? I'm not sure. Pulling my phone out of my pocket, I call Pops.

"Anything?" he asks.

"She came into the woods. Why didn't I think to check the goddamn fucking woods? Fuck. We need... I don't know... Get some choppers flying overhead, get every man we have available out here searching. She's in these woods somewhere," I tell him.

"Got it. Matteo, hold it together just a little longer. We're getting close. We will find her."

"It's not the *if* we're going to find her I'm worried about. It's the state she's going to be in when we do."

"Let's just find her," he says before ending the call with a click.

"It looks like she's crawled through here." The nameless guy points to a trail of crushed leaves.

"Why the fuck is she crawling?" I say out loud. Neither of them answer, not that I expected them too. The dogs follow the flattened path. We walk for another twenty minutes, going deeper into the woods, before they pause again. "Why are they stopping?" I ask.

"The trail ends. They've lost her scent," Jaxon says.

I look around, the crawl marks have stopped too. "Where could she have gone?"

"I don't know, man."

I'm looking around for any signs of someone else's presence when I see faint boot prints in the dirt. "Here. Someone walked here." I point to the markings.

They bring the dogs over to track the scent. "They're not hers."

"Fucking, fuck!" I grind out, pulling at my hair. "She has to be out here somewhere. Savvy!" I cup my hands around my mouth and start yelling. I continue to follow the footprints, calling out to her as I go. My throat is hoarse, but I'm not the only one yelling. I can hear all of my men echoing her name.

It's pitch-black now. I can barely see two feet in front of me. The light from three choppers flying overhead flicks across the ground.

I lean against a tree and close my eyes. "Where the fuck are you, Savannah?"

"Matteo, we need to go back to the house. Come on." Pops's no-nonsense voice makes my eyes pop open.

"I'm not leaving here without her," I tell him.

"There are a hundred men in these woods, each more equipped to find her right now than you are. Let them do their jobs," he says.

"I can't leave here without her."

"Okay, we'll keep going. Come on." He doesn't argue anymore, placing a hand on my shoulder as we walk side by side through the woods. Both calling out her name.

Family is everything to my father. I never doubted he'd always have my back, and right now it shows more than ever. He's our rock. He will never know how grateful I am to have him in my corner. To have him as my role model.

29

SAVVY

*Love must be sincere. Hate what is evil;
cling to what is good.*

Romans 12:9

The sound of machines beeping brings me back to consciousness. Where am I? My eyes slowly blink open, fighting the burn from the light. It's bright in here, really bright.

"You're awake?" a deep, husky voice says.

Turning my head, I'm greeted by a megawatt smile, all-white teeth, and dimples on a really handsome face. Do I know this person? Who is he?

"How you feeling?" the stranger asks again.

"Wh-wh—" I try to speak, but my throat is so dry I can't get the words out.

"Shit, sorry, hang on." He picks up a cup and walks closer to the bed. He points the straw in my direction. "Just take small sips," he says, placing the straw in my mouth.

The water is heavenly, the coolness soothing as it trickles down my throat. "Thank you," I say, in a still-raspy voice. My eyes roam the room. I'm in a hospital. At least I hope it's a hospital. "Are you a doctor?" I ask the tall, handsome stranger.

"Not yet. I'm a med student," he replies with a grin.

My eyebrows scrunch down in confusion. *Why is he here? Where's Matteo?*

"I found you in the woods. You weren't in too good of shape. I carried you out—thank God you're only a little thing." His dimples deepen.

"Matteo. Where's Matteo?" I ask.

"Ah, the infamous Matteo. You've been whispering his name in your sleep. Lucky guy. Does he have a last name? I can give him a call for you," he offers with an encouraging nod.

"How long have I been here?"

"Two days. The doctors were insistent that you'd wake up when your body was ready. You didn't have any ID on you. No phone, nothing."

"I-I need Matteo," I say.

"Do you know his number? You can use my phone if you want," he prompts.

"Thank you."

"No worries. I'll just step outside, give you some privacy." He reaches over and places a remote beside me on the bed. "Press the call button if you need anything."

"Wait!" I call out and he stops, just before he makes it to the door, and turns around. "Where am I?" I ask.

"You're at Mercy General." He smiles and exits.

I don't wait a moment longer to dial Matteo's number. The phone rings twice before he answers. "Yeah?" His voice is grating.

"Tao?"

There's a silence that passes over us before he speaks again. "Savvy? Thank fucking God. Where are you? Are you okay? I'm so fucking sorry. So sorry." I can hear the waves of emotion lacing his words through the phone.

"I'm at Mercy General. I'd really like it if you could come and get me," I tell him.

"I'm on my way. Don't move. Shit, are you okay? Where have you been? I've been going out of my damn mind looking for you."

"I'm okay. I just... I really need you, Tao."

"Not nearly as much as I need you," he says. "Christian, Mercy General, let's go." I hear him running, then a car start. "I'm on my way, Savvy. I'm coming."

"Thank you." I yawn. My head hurts, and I'm tired. My eyes start to close. He's coming for me. "Matteo, I love you," I tell him. "I'm really tired."

"Fuck, Christian, go faster," he yells. "Savvy, I love you. I'm fifteen minutes away. I'll be there before you know it."

"Okay, if I fall asleep, can you wake me up when you get here?"

"Of course."

My eyelids get heavier. I let them close.

"I promise, Savvy, I'm taking you away. We're getting away from here. I won't let anything like this happen to you again. I swear it."

"It's not your fault." *It's not. I mean that.*

"Yes, it is. I should have been there. I should have protected you better."

"It's okay. I'm okay. I just need to see your ridiculously pretty face." I smile, and the image of Matteo smiling back at me flits through my mind.

§⚭

"WHO THE FUCK are you and what the fuck are you doing with my wife?" Matteo's angry voice stirs me back to consciousness.

I slowly blink my eyes open. He's here. Matteo's here. "Tao?" I call for him.

"Don't fucking move," he says to the nice guy from before—the one who said he found me, who brought me here, and let me use his phone.

Why is Matteo angry at him?

"I'm right here, babe. I'm here." Matteo leans down,

peppering light kisses over my lips, before he moves along my neck towards my ear. "Fuck, I'm so sorry," he whispers.

"It's okay. I'm okay. Can you take me home now?" I ask him.

"Soon. I need to talk to your doctors." Matteo lifts his head. I watch his gaze shoot to the door where Christian is standing guard. "Get him out of here. Find out who the fuck he is," Matteo orders.

"Wait. Matteo, stop. He didn't do anything. He found me in the woods and brought me here," I explain.

"You've been gone for four days, Savvy," Matteo says.

"I know. When I woke up, the first thing I did was call you."

Matteo nods his head to Christian and waits for the room to empty. "I've never been so fucking scared in my life." Tears start to fall down his cheeks. I've only seen him cry a few times, and it absolutely breaks my heart.

"I'm sorry. I didn't know what to do." I reach up a hand, about to wipe his tears away, when I notice it's wrapped in a bandage.

Matteo gently takes hold of my wrist, kissing the exposed knuckles on my fingers. "It's not your fault. You never should have been in that situation." He takes a deep breath. "I need to know, Savvy. Did they...? What happened?"

"I don't know. All I remember is hearing gunshots and I was locked in the car. Rocco told me to wait. So I did. But then I heard the shots. I couldn't get out so I called Loch. He disarmed the system—do not get angry at him for that," I warn him.

"Wasn't planning on it, babe," he says. "What else?"

"I walked along the side of the house. I didn't know what to do, just that I had to get out of there. Someone came around the corner and he started running towards me. I didn't have a choice. I had to... I shot him. I don't know if he actually died? Oh my god, did I kill someone?" I ask suddenly.

"No, babe, you didn't kill anyone," Matteo says. He's lying. I can always tell when he's lying. Not many people can but I know. I appreciate him trying to hide that sin from me though. I smile weakly. I have the type of blood on my hands that will never wash off. "What happened after you shot the fucker?" Matteo grits his teeth with that last part. His jaw is tight, his eyes almost black.

"I ran. I just kept running. I didn't know if they were chasing me so I just kept running through the woods. It was stupid, I know."

"No, it was fucking smart, Savvy. You ran—that's exactly what you should have done."

"Rocco? Is he okay?" I finally bring myself to ask the question weighing heavily on my heart.

Matteo looks at the wall on the opposite side of the room. "No, he's gone," he says.

"I'm so sorry. I know how much you liked him."

"It's okay. I'm sorry I couldn't find you. We went into the woods. I haven't stopped looking, Savvy, I swear. I just pulled everyone back when I got your call. I would never stop looking for you."

"I know. Did you, ah, did you talk to Loch?" I ask him.

"Yes. Why?"

"Did he tell you?"

"Tell me what?"

"I asked him to tell you that I didn't want those papers anymore, Matteo. I wanted you to know, in case something happened to me. I love you. Am I scared of what the future holds? Yes, but I'm not going to let that take any more time away from us."

"You were never getting those papers anyway, babe. As much as I know that the right thing to do is let you go, I just can't fucking do it."

"Good, because I don't want you to."

The door opens and Matteo audibly growls at the interruption. "It seems you gave a lot of people a scare, Miss." An older man with a kind smile walks into the room, a pen in his shaky hand. He picks up the chart from the end of the bed.

"It's Missus," Matteo corrects him. "Mrs. Valentino."

"Right, Mrs. Valentino. I'm Dr. Johnson. How are you feeling?"

"Like I've been hit by a freight train," I say honestly.

"On a scale from one to ten, how much pain are you in?" he prods.

"Ah, five?" My answer comes out more like a question.

Matteo's body stiffens. "Savvy, answer truthfully. How much pain are you in?" he says. The thing about knowing each other like we do is that we can never get away with lying.

"Seven. But it's mostly my ankle," I clarify.

"That's not surprising. You have a trimalleolar fracture. The orthopedic surgeon will be down shortly to talk you through the surgery he performed on your ankle."

"Give her something for the pain. She shouldn't be in so much fucking pain," Matteo growls.

"We already have her on morphine. Your next dose is due in thirty minutes, Mrs. Valentino. The nurse will be in soon to check on you. I'm glad you're awake and feeling better," the doctor says. Not sure I'd agree that *feeling better* is all that accurate. I do feel more at ease, though, knowing Matteo is here.

"What the fuck? You expect her to just lie there in agony for thirty more fucking minutes? What kind of doctor are you? Actually, don't answer that. Because you're about to not be one at all." Matteo runs his hands through his already disheveled hair.

I peer up at him, take him in. I didn't notice it before but his face is scruffy and his eyes have dark circles around them. He looks like he hasn't slept in days. "Matteo, it's okay. Really. Please just sit back down," I plead with him.

"It's not okay, Savvy. You don't need to be in pain. I'm calling Doc." He takes his phone out of his pocket and dials.

"Right. I'll leave you to it. You have a number of people waiting to see you. Should I let them in?"

"Yes," I answer at the same time Matteo says, "No."

"Let them in please," I tell the doctor, trying to apologize with my eyes for my husband's behavior. I know Matteo is coming from a place of love and concern. He means well. He's also not used to people not asking *how high* whenever he says *jump*.

The door opens and the whole Valentino family piles in. Holly runs up to my bedside. "Oh my gosh, look at you. Jesus, I'm so sorry, Savannah." She leans down and gently hugs me. And I can't help it... Holly has always been a motherly figure to me, and when she finally wraps her arms around me, it's like the dam breaks and I just start crying.

"Fuck, You all need to get out. You're making her upset." Matteo's voice rises.

"No, it's okay. I'm just so happy to see you. All of you," I say.

"Savannah, is there anything you need? Anything at all. I'll make sure you get it." Mr. Valentino stands at the foot of the bed, his hands in his pockets. He's looking just as rough as Matteo.

My eyes travel to the other three Valentino brothers, presently filling the remainder of the space in the room—they all look like they could use a shower and a good meal. "You all look like crap," I say it aloud this time. "You need to go home, shower, eat, and sleep."

"I think you must have broken your eyesight along with that ankle, Savannah, because I never look anything less than devilishly handsome." Romeo winks at me.

Trust that boy to make me laugh. The worst bit about it is that I think he truly believes what he's saying. God help any girl who falls for him. I'm not sure how they'd ever keep up with the self-inflated ego he has going on.

"Of course you are. But you're also tired. I appreciate you all being here. For looking for me. For everything." I get choked up by my overwhelming gratitude.

"Savannah, you're family. There is nowhere else we'd be." This comes from Theo—Theo, the usually strong, brooding, silent one. Although I've third-wheeled his and Matteo's outings enough to know he's way more than just the grump he likes to portray himself to be.

"Thank you."

30

MATTEO

The art of war is of vital importance to the State. It is a matter of life and death, a road either to safety or to ruin.

— Sun Tzu, The Art of War

It took an hour but I finally got everyone to leave. Savannah fell asleep again after the nurse came in and administered her dose of morphine. She looks peaceful. I can't stop staring at her.

"I've arranged for a bed to be set up in here for you, Mr. Valentino," a young nurse says as a couple of orderlies wheel it in before positioning it next to Savvy's.

"Thank you," I tell her. I have no intention of sleeping. All I want to do is sit here and watch my wife. I just want to thank God that she's okay. That she's with me again and beg him to never let us be apart again.

I know Pops finished off the Russian we had tied up in the basement. Theo pulled me aside and said that Petrov had ordered his men to burn my house. The guys we caught up with, the ones in the SUVs, were nothing more than low-level soldiers.

I don't know what the fuck this Petrov fucker is playing at; however, I do know it's a game he won't fucking win. I have no doubt this war with the Russians is far from over. When the orderlies and the nurse leave the room, I open the door and peek outside. And sure enough, Christian is standing guard. "Go home, Christian. Get some sleep," I tell him.

"It's fine, boss. I'd rather stay," he says.

I shrug. *Stubborn bastard.* "Fine. What'd you get out of him?" I ask, referring to the kid we found in Savvy's hospital room when we arrived.

"He's a med student at NYU. Clean as a whistle. On a scholarship. He checks out," he says.

"So he's just some good Samaritan, who found Savvy and carried her God knows how many miles through the woods?" I say.

"It seems that way."

"Yeah, keep an eye on him. Trust no one, Christian. I don't believe in coincidences. What was he doing in the woods in the first place?"

"Says he was hiking."

"Right. A scholarship kid, hiking through the forest

surrounding one of the wealthiest neighborhoods in the area. Who the fuck is he? Little Red Riding Hood? Next you're going to tell me unicorns fucking exist." I roll my eyes. *Fucking hiking.*

"I'll keep digging." Christian looks past me and into the room. "How is she?"

"She's okay. She's going to be okay." I sigh. "Thank you for everything. I won't ever forget it, Christian."

"Sure, anytime. I'm going to go get some coffee. You want anything?" he offers.

"Nah, I'm good." I wave him off, closing the door as I go and sit in the chair next to Savvy's bed. Then I rest my forehead on the edge, while my hand wraps around her arm.

I should never have taken those damn cuffs off. I should just chain her to my side 24/7. I wonder if she'd let me... I chuckle at how well *that* conversation would go down. There's one thing I need to do—something I should have done hours ago.

I press the *call* button next to the name of the one person in the world I fucking despise but can't do a damn thing about.

"Hello, Matteo, what's happened?" The voice on the other end confuses me. There's genuine concern there and it doesn't feel right.

"Mr. St. James. I'm, ah, just calling to let you know Savvy was in an accident. She's okay but I just thought you'd want to know."

"What kind of accident? Where is she?"

"She's at Mercy General. She's okay—a broken ankle but other than that, she's fine. I just… I'll get her to call you herself when she wakes up," I tell him.

"She's okay? Are you sure?"

"Yes."

"You're there with her?" he asks.

"There's nowhere else I'd be." I know he hates me. He's always hated our friendship, his daughter's ties to me. I wonder if now's a good time to let him know we're officially more than that. That there is no getting rid of me.

I decide against it. That's something Savvy should choose for herself. If she wants him to know, she'll tell him. I couldn't, in good conscience, keep this from him though—the fact that his daughter is lying in a hospital bed is something he should know. I'd like to think, if I had a daughter in a similar situation, that someone would give me that same courtesy. It'd mean a slow death—all-out war for whomever put her there. But that goes without saying.

The thought of having mini Savvys brings a smile to my face. I wonder if she'd be keen on building our own little family sooner rather than later. I can't wait to have it all with her.

"Thank you for letting me know. Please tell Savannah to call me," he says.

"Sure." I hang up, having completed my good deed for the day. Though I'm no less confused by his mannerisms and tone. He sounded almost… sober. Has he finally cleaned up his act? I really fucking hope for Savvy's sake he has. She won't admit it, but I know it hurts her not having her own family involved in her life.

"Mmm, Matteo?" And just like that, her sleepy voice is music to my ears.

"I'm right here, babe," I tell her, leaning forward to kiss her forehead.

"Don't leave me," she says.

"Never. Go back to sleep. I'll be right here when you wake up."

❧

FEATHERLIGHT TOUCHES RUN down my cheek. I jump up, startled, and quickly scan the room.

"Sorry, I didn't mean to wake you," Savvy says.

"Are you okay?" I ask her.

"Uh-huh. I could use some water. Coffee would be even better."

"Here, drink this." I hand her a cup. She takes it with her unbandaged hand—a hand that shakes to the point I have to cover it with my own to steady her. My eyebrows draw down. "What's wrong? Are you in pain?"

"No, I'm okay."

"Don't lie to me, Savvy. What's going on?"

"I just… I had a nightmare. I was back in the woods,

except I didn't make it out. He found me. The man I shot found me." Her voice quivers.

"He can't hurt you anymore, Savvy. I promise."

"I know. It was just a nightmare. I'm okay, Matteo, promise."

"I love you. So damn much." I press my cheek against her forehead.

"I know." She smiles.

"I was thinking last night… How soon can we start our family?"

"What do you mean?" she asks, suddenly sitting up straighter.

"I want more of you, Savvy. I'm selfish, and I want a house filled with mini Savannahs."

"You want a house full of daughters?" She quirks a brow at me.

"Why wouldn't I? You're fucking perfect. Our daughters will be just as perfect." My lips tip up at the image.

"I feel like you haven't really thought this through too well, Tao. You do know that girls like me… date boys like you. You want the type of daughters who fall in love with the bad boy and follow him around everywhere, hoping he's going to notice her?"

My head tilts to the side. "There hasn't been a day I haven't noticed you, babe. Besides, our daughters will be nuns. There won't be any boyfriends," I tell her with a definitive nod.

See? I have already thought this through.

"Right, I'm not sure you get to decide that."

"We'll see. So how soon?"

"How about we just let nature take its course and see what happens," she says. "We also need to buy a new house."

"Consider it done. Where do you want to live?"

"Somewhere close to your parents. If we're having a house load of kids, we're going to want to be able to send them over to their grandparents. A lot." Savvy's laughter fills the room.

"Deal." I lean down and seal our plan with a kiss. "I called your dad last night. He'd like you to call him this morning," I tell her.

"You called my dad? Why?"

"Savvy, you're in a hospital bed, hurt. He has a right to know."

"I must say I have to agree with you on that, Matteo." My shoulders stiffen at the sound of the voice that just entered the room.

Savvy gasps. "Dad? What are you doing here?" she asks.

"Your friend called me and said you were in an accident. I came to see for myself that you're okay. How are you feeling?"

Have I woken up in an alternate universe? Since when does Mr. St. James care if Savvy is okay or not? He's usually too deep into a bottle of Jack to care about much of anything.

"I'm okay. You didn't have to come all this way."

"Yes, I did. Is there anything you need? What are the doctors saying?"

"It's just a broken ankle—that's all," Savvy replies. "Matteo, can you get me that coffee, please?"

I give her the *you're out of your damn mind if you think I'm leaving this room* look. "Sure, hold on." Opening the door, I find Christian sitting on the floor. "Can you get Savvy a coffee, vanilla creamer?" I hold out a hundred-dollar bill.

"Yep, won't be long." He doesn't take my cash, just pushes to his feet and pivots down the hallway towards the cafeteria.

I walk back to Savvy's bedside. "Christian is getting it for you, babe." I smile down at her. She rolls her eyes at me.

"I, ah, I'm sober, Savannah. Have been for six months." Mr. St. James looks down at the floor as he says this. "I know I've fucked up. I know I've hurt you. I also know I can't take back the things I've said. I can't make up for the years of your childhood I ruined."

"Dad, it's okay…"

"No, it's not. But I want to make it okay. I want to… would it be all right if I visited every now and then?"

"Sure." Savvy turns to me, and we share *a what the actual fuck* look.

"I have this for you. Your mother wanted you to have this on your wedding day." He passes her an envelope. "I'll leave you to it. I'm glad you're okay, Savannah."

"Thank you." She hasn't taken her eyes off the envelope in her hand. "How did you know?" she asks him.

"I got a notification for your change of name on your trust," he says.

"My trust? I never…" Savvy looks to me, then rolls her eyes.

"You're welcome." I wink at her. I'm sure this isn't the last I'll hear of this conversation.

"Thanks, Dad."

"Of course. Call me if you need anything." Mr. St. James stands awkwardly at the end of the bed before turning and exiting the room.

Christian walks in with a coffee and a paper bag in his hand. "Morning, Mrs. Valentino. Coffee with vanilla creamer and a blueberry muffin. I hope you're feeling better, ma'am," he says, placing the items on the little bedside table.

"Thank you, Christian, and it's just Savannah. Not ma'am, not Mrs. Valentino, just Savannah."

He nods and quickly leaves the room.

"Matteo?"

"Yeah?"

"Take me home. Get me out of this hospital please," she pleads with me.

"I'd be glad to." I lean down and claim her lips with mine again.

EPILOGUE

MATTEO

Six months later

I've gone to war for my family more times than I can count, over territories, deals, and wrongdoings. I will go down fighting, if that's what it takes to make sure the Valentinos are always the ones coming out on top.

Never have I faced a war with the stakes as high as those of the past twelve months. In every war, there's a losing side and a winning side. In the battle for Savvy's heart, I was always only going to be the victor. Losing that battle was never an option.

I reap the benefits every morning I get to wake up

next to her. Every day I get to spend with her. Six months ago, I thought I'd lost her. I thought I'd lost my whole reason for living. I never want to endure that again. It took three months of healing and rehabilitation before she was cleared by the doctors. All that's left of the ordeal are the tiny scars from the surgery on her ankle, and the internal scars we both share. The ones no one can see.

Savannah might have stopped asking for divorce papers, but I haven't stopped proving to her every day that we're meant to be. That there was never a destiny where we didn't end up together. I've known since I was six years old that this girl was special. That knowledge hasn't dimmed, only grown tenfold. She's not just special; she's fucking phenomenal. In fact, I might just get a taste of her phenomenalism for breakfast.

Rolling over, I find her side empty. Damn it, I hate it when she gets up before me. Maybe I need to revisit the handcuff idea. Rolling out of the bed, I walk into the closet and find a pair of workout shorts. I run a hand through my hair and stretch out my tired muscles as I make my way through the house, looking for my wife. I ensured Savvy got her dream home, one near my parents' estate. She's done an exceptional job furnishing the place. There are perks to being married to an interior designer. Our house looks like it stepped right out of a magazine.

"Savvy, you and your pretty little pussy need to get here and let me eat my breakfast. I'm starved," I call out as I enter the kitchen. I look to Savvy, whose face is now beetroot red. Then I glance at the cause of her embarrassment. Romeo, Luca, and Livvy are sitting at the counter. "What the fuck are you all doing here?" I growl at them. The thing about living so close to my parents, the thing I didn't think through, is that my family seems to be of the opinion that our house is the latest drop-in center. They're always fucking here.

"Good to see you too, bro." Luca laughs.

Shaking my head, I ignore Thing One, Thing Two, and the way-too-sweet Livvy. I wrap my arms around Savvy. "I'm going to need you to come back to bed, babe," I whisper in her ear.

"Mmm, tempting. Rain check?" she asks, pulling back.

I roll my eyes. I don't want a rain check. I want her now. I send my brothers a glare, which only makes them both laugh at me. Little shits know they're cock-blocking me.

"We can come back later. We didn't mean to disturb you guys." This comes from Livvy. Like I said, she's way too sweet for the likes of my brother, who's staring at her with stars in his eyes.

"Doll, he will survive one morning without getting his dick wet. Trust me," Romeo says to her, making her whole body turn red. She averts her eyes, unable to look at me.

Pivoting back to Savvy, I cup her cheeks and fuse my lips with hers. My tongue delves into her mouth.

She tastes of coffee and vanilla. "Good morning,. How are you feeling?" I ask Savvy.

"I'm good, really good. But hungry, so stop bothering me so I can finish cooking breakfast." She waves a hand over the stove and I see three separate pans: one with bacon, one with blueberry pancakes, and one with chocolate chip pancakes. The twins' favorites.

"Go sit down. I'll finish this," I tell her. My hands land on her shoulders and I walk her around the counter. I pull a stool out and land another kiss to the top of her head. Returning to the stove, I flip the pancakes and call over my shoulder, "Come out with it already. Why are you here? And for future reference, my wife isn't your damn cook. You can both make your own damn pancakes." I point the spatula at Romeo and Luca.

"Livvy has an essay for school she wanted you to read over," Romeo says.

"It's okay. You don't have to. I know you're really busy and all," Livvy says, refusing to meet my eyes. Romeo, however, uses his to plead with me.

"What's it about? I love essays," I lie, trying to put the poor girl at ease.

"Ah, it's a comparative analysis of policing models: mafia to organized crime," Livvy says quietly.

I can't help but laugh. "So you thought you'd come straight to the source, huh?" I ask her.

"I, ah, it's already written, but I just want someone to read it." She looks at Romeo. "Someone who isn't *him*, because he just says everything I write is great, which isn't the truth," she's quick to add.

"Doll, it *is* the fucking truth. You're a little genius in pretty wrapping. It's a crime in itself really. Smart chicks aren't supposed to be hot too." His eyes roam up and down the length of her.

"Okay, Romeo, keep it in your pants." I turn back and remove the pancakes from the pans, loading them up onto plates. Savvy has a bowl of scrambled eggs, a plate of assorted bagels and breads, and another plate of freshly cut fruit—all sitting on the counter. How long has she been awake?

"You two, make yourselves useful and carry these to the table," I direct to Romeo and Luca. "Livvy, send me your essay. I can't wait to read it," I tell her honestly. It does sound interesting, and I'm intrigued by what her thoughts are on the topic.

"Thank you, I appreciate it." She smiles.

"You really are punching above your paygrade with that one, Romeo," I tell him, dropping a plate of pancakes in front of him.

"I know." He grins wide and proud.

TWO HOURS. That's how long it took me to get the twins to leave my fucking house. I made them both clean up after breakfast while Savvy and I spoke to

Livvy about her essay. That girl is smart, probably the only thing she and Romeo actually have in common.

Finally, I get Savvy to myself. Taking her hand, I'm about to lead her back upstairs to the bedroom, but I don't have that kind of time to waste. My cock's been aching for her since I woke up. So, instead, I guide her into the living room.

"I thought they'd never leave," I tell her. She's wearing a sundress. Reaching my hands up and under the hem, I find the top of her panties and drag the thin material down her legs.

She steps out of them, kicking the fabric to the side. "Well, now that you have me all to yourself, what are you going to do to me?" Her eyes gloss over with desire.

I step back. "First, I'm going to lick that glorious pussy of yours until your juices are flowing down my throat. Then, I'm going to bend you over and bury my cock so deep inside you you'll be begging for mercy."

Savvy bites her lip. "Why would I beg for something I know you don't give."

"Oh. you'll beg," I tell her, pushing her down on the sofa and kneeling between her legs. "Are you wet for me, Savvy? Am I going to put my tongue into you and taste that sweet nectar?"

"Y-yes," she stammers as I spread her legs wide, running my tongue up the inside of her thighs until I reach the motherland.

I glide my tongue through her slick folds. "Fuck yes,

this is what I'm talking about." I dive back in, licking, sucking, nibbling on her.

"Oh shit, Tao, please, I'm going to…" Her words trail off.

My palm roams upwards until I find her breast, rolling one taught nipple between my fingertips. Savvy's hands yank at my hair. I'm not sure if she's trying to pull me away or push me closer to her pussy. Her hips are grinding upwards into me. I tug harder at her nipple, twisting a little as my mouth sucks on her engorged clit. That's all it takes to send her soaring. Her legs tighten around my head, locking me in place as she rides out her orgasm. I continue to lick her until she's fully relaxed. Until her head lolls back and her eyes close. Standing upright, I grab the waistband of my shorts and start pulling them down.

"Matteo, Savvy, you here?" my mother's voice calls out.

"Fuck, what the fuck is it with my family and cock-blocking me?" I drag my shorts back up, my boner fucking destroyed by the sound of my mother's voice. Savvy laughs as she pushes to her feet, plucks her panties from the floor, and shoves them between the crack in the sofa cushions. "We're changing the locks," I tell her.

"Sure we are." She laughs again, walking out of the living room while leaving me alone with my fucking blue balls.

EPILOGUE

SAVVY

Four years later

I stare at the stick—the one with two pink lines. How the hell did I let him do this to me again? My mind plays through a collage of images of Matteo and me fucking. I smile. *I know how.* That man is a damn god at what he does.

Lorenzo our son is two, and Enzo, our other son is five months old. Yes, I let Matteo name them. I'm pretty sure I was still high on pain relief when I signed those birth certificate forms. Now I'm pregnant again. I really need to learn how to resist Matteo's charms.

"Babe, you okay?" The doorknob rattles as Matteo tries to get into the bathroom.

"Yep, I'll be out in a sec," I say, wiping the tears from my cheeks. I'm not sure if these are tears of happiness, distress, or just plain exhaustion. Because I'm tired. Anyone who tells you that motherhood is all glorious and happy moments is straight bullshitting you. It's not an Instagram account full of photogenic moments. It's sleepless nights, vomit-covered clothing, the death of whatever social life you had. And yet, when I look into the faces of my baby girls, I wouldn't give them up for the world.

"Open the door, Savvy," Matteo hisses through the door. The boys have just fallen asleep, and he knows if he wakes them, they're all his problem. Not that he'd complain. I swear he wakes them up on purpose just so he has an excuse to hold them longer.

I used to think Matteo couldn't possibly get any sexier. That was until I saw him with our sons. That man, bare-chested with a baby lying on him, makes my ovaries swoon. Apparently literally too, considering my current predicament.

"Please, God, let it just be one this time." I send up a little prayer. Taking a huge breath, I wipe at my cheeks a second time and open the door.

Matteo is standing on the other side. His face drops when he sees me. "What's wrong?" he asks. I hand him the stick and he looks down at it. Silence encompasses us for a few moments before he looks back up at me again, his own eyes shining with unshed tears. "We're having another baby?" he attempts to clarify.

"Looks that way." I smile.

Throwing the stick over his shoulder, he picks me up and my legs wrap around his waist. "I'm so fucking happy, babe. We're getting another one. Another piece of you and me," he says, slamming his lips onto mine.

I tug at his hair and pull his face back. "Those boys are all you and you know it."

"Doesn't matter, if it's a boy or a girl. It'll be perfect either way. We make perfect fucking babies." He grins.

"We do," I agree.

Matteo walks us over to the bed, and laying me down way more gently than he did just last night, he yanks at the string holding my robe in place. "Una fottuta bellezza senza sforzo," he says as he takes in the sight of me. All of me.

At first, after I had Lorenzo I was self-conscious about my changing body. My stomach isn't as flat as it once was, now decorated with stretch marks—which Matteo refers to as beauty marks. He really helped me love myself again. His unwavering devotion to me, the fact that he still gets turned on by me, that we can walk into a room full of supermodels and he still only looks at me… That kind of love goes beyond appearances. It's soul-deep.

I knew from a very young age that he was the one my soul loved. I wasted so much time being afraid of ruining our friendship, our connection, that I didn't consider how much stronger it could be. If I'd just given in...

Being with Matteo, letting go of my fears, has only made us better. I can't think of anyone else I'd rather spend the rest of my life with than my best friend.

...I have found the one whom my soul loves...

Song of Solomon 3:4

ACKNOWLEDGMENTS

First, I'd like to acknowledge you, the reader. The person who read through Matteo and Savvy's book from start to end. Who lived in the world of the Valentino's for a short period of time and become part of the family. I would not be here, continuing these amazing worlds with characters that speak to my heart and hopefully yours, without your continued support.

I'd like to thank my Patron members, who continue to keep my spirits lifted with their faith and belief in my words. Tawny, Megan, Juliet, Jenna, Monique, Kayla, Sam, Chris, Amber and Michelle. Thank you, thank you thank you for everything!!

My beta readers, Vicki, Amy, Melissa and Sam, you are all priceless. Matteo and Savvy's journey would not be the same without you.

My content designer Assunta, you are an absolute gem!! Without you, not half as many people would know the Valentino Sons, thank you for the amazing content and keeping my socials looking as fab as they do!

My editor, Kat, the one who polishes the story to make it the best it can possibly be. I could not do this without her—if I could lock her in my basement and keep her editing for me only, for the rest of her days, I would! Maybe I should ask Matteo to arrange this for me.

I have to thank Sammi B, from Sammi Bee Designs, the amazingly talented cover designer, who worked tire-lessly on the beautiful covers for the Sons of Valentino Series.

ABOUT KYLIE KENT

Kylie is a hopeless romantic with a little bit of a dark and twisted side. She loves love, no matter what form it comes in. Sweat, psychotic, stalkerish it doesn't matter as long as the story ends in a happy ending and tons of built in spice.

There is nothing she loves doing more than getting lost in a fictional world, going on adventures that only stories can take you.

Kylie loves to hear from her readers; you can reach her at: author.kylie.kent@gmail.com

For a complete reading order visit

Visit Kylie's website : www.kyliekent.com

Printed in Great Britain
by Amazon

35747305R00149